The Woman Who

Dared

Touch Jesus

Ginger Tsang

This is a work of fiction. Although based on stories found in the Bible, the events and characters described here are products of the author's imagination.

Ginger Tsang
Visit my website at www.gingertsang.com
Printed in the United States of America
First Printing: December 2008
ISBN-13 978-0-578-00046-6

For all the WONDERFUL ladies in my life, Grama Bell,
Momuski, Robin, and my daughters
Crystal, and Isabelle.

ACKNOWLEDGEMENTS

I WOULD LIKE to thank my husband Derick for being the best soundboard a first-time writer ever had on ideas and first draft editing! You helped me find those impossible pockets of uninterrupted time to work on this novel. In addition, your expertise in setting up my website www.gingertsang.com was just plain outstanding. Thanks hun, ABILWU.

Special thanks to my sister. Robin, who worked diligently to meet my editing deadline despite a hectic schedule. Through the years, I've enjoyed all the hours of laughter we've shared and I look forward to many more! "Cup" on over anytime, sis!

Thanks to Dee Byers at the Springwater Library in Midhurst, who ceaselessly ordered and processed the many requests I made during my research, and the whole team of wonderful ladies: Senga Coutts, Kathy Cook, Maggie Sparrow, Lesley Heaslip, Marg O'Neill, Elisa

Rice, Carol Grenier and Lynn Patkau who make all three library locations, Midhurst, Elmvale and Minesing such great, positive places.

Thanks to my trio of amazing ladies at PT, Stephanie DeRosa, Danielle Feudale and Alisha Leonard who could always be depended upon for their fresh perspectives, comments, suggestions and encouragement in my writing of this story.

Thanks also to the team of great employees at Lulu.com who helped make my dream a reality in your hands.

Now a woman who had the hemorrhage for twelve years, and had spent all her wealth for doctors, could not be healed by anybody. She came near him from behind, and touched the edge of his cloak; and immediately her hemorrhage stopped. And Jesus said, 'Who touched me?' And when all of them denied it, Simon Peter and those who were with him said to him, 'Teacher, the crowds are troubling you and pressing on you, and yet you say, 'Who has touched me?' But he said, 'Some one has touched me, for I know that power has gone out of me.' When the woman saw that she could not deceive him, she came trembling, and fell down and worshipped him; and she said in the presence of all the people for what purpose she had touched him, and how she was healed immediately. Jesus said to her, 'Have courage my daughter; your faith has healed you; go in peace.'

Luke 8:43-48

And behold a woman who had had the hemorrhage for twelve years, came up from behind him, and she touched the edge of his cloak; For she was saying to herself, 'If I can only touch his garment, I will be healed.' And Jesus turned around and saw her and said to her, 'Have courage, my daughter, your faith has healed you'; and the woman was healed in that very hour.

Matthew 9:20-22

And there was a woman who had had the hemorrhage for twelve years, who had suffered much at the hands of many doctors, and had spent everything she had, and was not helped at all, but rather became worse. When she heard concerning Jesus, she came through the dense crowd from behind him, and touched his cloak. For she said, 'If I can only touch his cloak, I will live.' And immediately the hemorrhage was dried up; and she felt in her body that she was healed of her disease.

Mark 5:25-29

The Woman Who
Dared
Touch Jesus

Each breath is a beginning
Each step is a learning
Each beat of my heart is
Yearning
for God

CHAPTER ONE

This is a story of courage. At the time, I did not think of myself as the courageous type, but desperation can drive us to heights beyond even our own imaginings. I used to think I understood the amount of pain I could handle. If you think for a moment, there are parameters in your mind, of your own emotional and physical boundaries. Now think of those boundaries being reached, then breached. How would you react? How much can your soul truly endure? In my experience, it was there, beyond those safe boundaries that I found God and my true self.

To tell you of my life, I first draw from a palette of happy colors that are bright and warm. Most don't remember my name, but it was Elishva, translated as Elisabeth in your English language. I was born in the year 9 CE at the cusp of a rising moon that marked a new month in our Jewish calendar. Not only was it a new moon, I was born at the beginning of the month of April, the fullest season of springtime. It's a time of new life when beauty bursts upon the land, energetic from its winter rest. Flowers of purple, yellow and blue contrasted with the varying greens against the brown/gray landscape of greater Judea. The wind carried my first cries to tickle those colorful flowers and brought a swinging smile to the grasses. "It has begun!" they sang to each other, as they sing for each birth of God's children.

The timing of my birth boded well for a life of promise I was told. Great things would come of my life the villagers foretold, but great also was the price I paid.

I was the eldest and only daughter in a family of three children. Just over a year after me, mother gave birth to my brother, Asher. Then, after an absence of pregnancies for 3 years, she gave birth to my younger brother, Yakhub. Unfortunately, Yakhub was the last child born to my mother. She would have liked more children, but she endured two miscarriages instead and then her womb was forever silent.

I was a Jew born in a land under the heavy thumb of the Roman Empire, and so, life tasted of salt. We could live in our holy land, indeed, but we could not rule it nor stop the Hellenistic Greeks and Romans from defiling that holy land. They built their gymnasiums for naked wrestling matches and running. In addition, they taxed our income unfairly, wore their emblem of Caesar on their armor offending everyone with this display of idolatry and as much as they tried to make a happy soup of us all, we were the salt that never mixed happily. Judea was inhabited with a dangerous mix of very different religions.

Of my childhood, I remember being loved and loving my parents deeply. There were hugs and laughter, sibling fights and tears that got kissed away. There was patience and smiles and always, there was love. I remember playing games with my brothers – days that were magically carefree. I would like to think that everyone has at least some portion of his or her childhood with such special times.

Being the eldest, I would naturally mother my younger brothers. But Asher, only a year younger than me, soon grew taller, and felt his status as firstborn son far outweighed my nurturing nuisances. Asher and Yakhub would always be play-fighting and I would always be trying to make peace. Granted, I must admit, I had my troubles with Asher too. He used to delight in sneaking up on me and pinching the soft skin on the back of my arm for no reason other than to see me wince! "Got you again, Elishva!" he would taunt. I'm sure it was never in retribution for the salt I used to sneak into his lambskin of water when he would go to the synagogue for his lessons....!

My brothers attended class six days a week at our synagogue to learn the Hebrew language and alphabet, memorize passages and stories from the five books of Moses.

Girls were not to be educated, so I stayed home with my mother. When the men would go to synagogue after supper, the women and young girls gathered in various homes in the evenings. While the married women talked, the young women listened and the girls played quietly. Beyond discussions of what had happened that day, there were debates about a woman's place in society and finding God in everything. They were seeking God from a woman's perspective and talking about the women who had helped shape the history of our people.

My favorite day of the week was naturally, the Sabbath, when we wore our neatest, cleanest clothes. After our family meal, my father would begin telling grand stories of the historic struggles of the Jewish people centuries before us. My father had a wonderful voice and captivated each of us with every word he spoke. The light of the flame from our oil lantern would contrast with the dark shadows of night on my father's face. Once, the light played tricks with my eyes and I felt stark fear when I thought his short beard was on fire! I was right in one sense, my father had the fire of our people's determination and a passion for righteousness that he wanted passed down to each of his children.

Noah's ark was a captivating story, but my favorite of all was the story of Moses. Even though I had heard it many times, I always held my breath when father got to the part where Moses touched the ground with his staff and the great waves separated. I could not imagine the courage it would take to have risked running along that ocean bottom, to flee from Egypt and everything they knew! *How terrifying it must have been! Terrifyingly glorious for our people! What an awesome God was ours!*

As my brothers learned more at school, they were asked to add to stories or discuss the different laws. The laws were so numerous, over six hundred in all. I often found debates over their details confusing and preferred by far the stories they would tell instead.

In contrast to my boisterous brothers, I was the quiet one. I kept my thoughts silent instead of voicing them to others. It wasn't because I lacked confidence; I simply kept my own counsel, and was rarely at odds with anyone. My mind and thoughts were like an olive grove. They were neat, orderly and fertile, but nothing fantastical. They had their purpose and their place was in silent growing.

Life had its order too. Every morning I went with my mother, aunt and cousins to the village well to help carry water. There were close to two hundred people living in our small village, and secrets didn't stay secrets for long! Mornings at the well were a fun time for me. All the young girls played while our mothers drew water and traded gossip.

Water was very important in our daily lives. There was water at the doors in large jars for those entering to wash their hands and feet. Water was also used in the house constantly, for washing in general before food preparation, eating, mending etc. It might seem odd that for so much water around, we never drank it! Our main liquid was wine. Although water was used mostly for the purpose of cleaning ourselves, after June, water was used to dilute wine. By then, the wine was old, and its bitterness had grown quite strong since its September harvest.

It was at the well one morning that I first left a piece of my childhood behind me forever. That fateful morning, I was playing with some girls and the conversation came to the topic of marriage. Sometimes we liked to pretend we were beautiful brides with flower wreaths in our hair for our wedding night banquet. One of my friends, a sweet child named Rachel, asked me about my older cousin Miriam's engagement to be married to a young man on my father's side of the family! I certainly hadn't heard this news, but Rachel wasn't a liar, and it scared me. *Miriam? My beloved Miriam? It couldn't be!* A distant cousin would mean she'd move away from me. But my heart shouted with the truth through my terror.

I ran scared from the village center. I quickly dashed along the narrow alleyways and made certain that I did not take the one where my father's business was located. I ran past all the familiar family compounds until I reached ours. Tears were stinging my eyes as I barreled past Miriam and Grandmother grinding barley in the compound entryway. I swiped once at my tears as I passed the entrances to all the dwellings, but gave up at that futile effort once I reached the open courtyard. The chickens scattered, squawking their upset at my disturbance. I scrambled over the gate leading to the stall for our goats, sheep and lambs. I huddled down in the corner, oblivious to the protests of our animals, and bawled into my knees.

It was a crushing reality that I, too, would soon grow up and leave my family home. It wasn't fair! It just wasn't fair! Even marrying into your own family did not guarantee that things would be the same. And I wanted things to stay the same.

Playing marriage was worlds away from it invading my space and those I loved so dearly! It hurt that nobody in my family had told me Miriam was engaged. Everyone knew how close we were. She might be my cousin, but in my heart, she was my big sister. Miriam was leaving, my beloved Miriam! Wrapped in a tight ball against the wall, I sobbed. At that moment in my life, I lost a piece of my childhood and I mourned its loss as dearly as one can at that age.

Miriam was the one that came to me. She wondered if I was upset over a nasty fight with Asher, but no. "Miriam!" I cried, "It is Rachel! She said you are engaged!"

"What of it, Elishva?" asked Miriam in her quiet manner.

"Engaged, Miriam! Engaged to be MARRIED? You would leave me?" I cried to her as if she had not understood the impact of the word "engaged".

"Elishva, all of us must marry. It is the natural course of life." Miriam was not surprised by my upset and felt badly that her quietly negotiated marriage contract had reached my ears this way.

"But, Miriam," I continued, "You will leave our village! I cannot think of you leaving everything you know!" In my childish way, I wanted to show her what a disadvantage it would be for HER to leave ME. Wasn't she scared to leave this village? Wasn't she scared to leave our family compound, everyone and everything so dear and familiar to her? Miriam sighed and rubbed my back for a moment and let me cry all the tears I had. "Elishva," Miriam's voice came soft and tender, as you would speak to a wounded animal. "You know it is the way of our women. It is the way of every woman to marry and have children, otherwise, who would take care of her in her old age? You don't want me to grow old and be a woman on my own, do you?" asked Miriam.

"No," I sniffed.

"Then life moves me to my next journey and you must be happy for me! It is in the happiness of those around us that we find strength to do what we must," explained Miriam. I looked up into her dark, olive eyes and through the haze of my tears I concentrated hard on seeing her, truly seeing my beloved cousin. The oval of her face and the gentle and encouraging smile she was giving me. The dark hair, barely visible at the hem of her head cloth and the small scar at the right side of her chin she'd gotten as a child when she fell and hit the well. She was so wonderful to me, so dear to my heart and in my eyes, very brave.

In comparison to her quiet strength, I felt small and sorry that I had run away when Rachel told me the news. I realized, for the first time in my life, I was being a big baby. My outburst must also have caused my mother concern, for if she did not see me run away, she would be looking for me soon to return home with the water.

I lifted my head and looked Miriam in the eye. My beloved Miriam, how my heart did break! I decided I had to be strong for her. "I will go back now," I solemnly informed her. Miriam smiled, nodded and patted my head in the old familiar way. So much a second mother to me, I desperately wanted her to be proud of me. So I stood, brushed the straw from my tunic and wiped my streaked face with the ends my soft, blue head cloth. Resolutely, I held my tears as I climbed over the gate and headed back towards the village well. If it must be so, then I must be happy for my Miriam.

I was thinking so intently on what I would say to encourage her and show my support, I unconsciously chose a path that led me past my father's business. My father was a proud nappah – a blacksmith, as was his father before him. The sharp Ping! Ping! Ping, of his hammer danced across my thoughts and startled me from my musings. "Elishva!" called my father. "Why are you not at the well with your mother? Wait a moment!" with a few more expert pings,

Father set the iron shape in the coals to keep warm while he came to speak with me. "I am outside for a moment!" he shouted to his brother, also working with a piece of iron. Despite rubbing my face, Father saw I had been crying and knelt down so we were nose to nose. "Elishva – is it your mother?" he asked, with a tremor in his voice. I shook my head no and his relief was like a comforting wave. *Maybe Miriam's husband will care about her as much as my father cares for my mother*, I thought. "Then what is causing your tears today?" he asked.

"Miriam..," I began, but my lip trembled and suddenly my emotions burst forth like a mighty waterfall. "Miriam is engaged, Papa! She is leaving me!" I tried to hold my trembles inside but I quaked with pain. Papa picked me up in a great, big bear hug and I drew comfort in the firm strength of his huge, warm hand that cupped almost the entire back of my head. "Elishva," he sighed. And I knew by his tone that he knew of Miriam's marriage and scolded me all at once.

"Papa, Papa, I am scared for her to leave," I whispered.

"Elishva. My quiet, little Elishva," my father thought to himself, *"how will I bear your own leaving in a few short years?"*

"Elishva," said Papa, setting me down eventually. "Is your mother not happily married?" he asked.

"Oh Papa, of course she is happy with you!" I exclaimed.

"Then why would Miriam not also deserve this happiness?" he asked.

"She deserves it," I whispered, "but I will miss her."

"I know," said father.

"Elishva!" I heard the relieved cry of my mother and turned to see her hurrying down the alley without the jugs.

In the busyness of our household, it was rare to have both parents to yourself and their combined comfort and muted tones as they spoke above my head soothed my broken heart. There was stability to be found in my world. Miriam might go, but my parents remained. Asher and Yakub remained. But the vibrant colors of my life seemed to fade a bit after Miriam married and moved away.

My home was a compound filled with the members of our family and my uncle's family. There were eleven of us living in small family quarters all joined by an open courtyard. At the farthest end of the courtyard were the animal's quarters. They were built at the eastern most position for both sounds and smells to be carried away on the breeze. We had five chickens that ran freely in the courtyard. In the pen were three goats for milk and I remember one very prosperous year, we even bought a calf in preparation for the Passover feast!

Between the various family members, the chores were divided among us as equally as possible. There was bread to be made each day, which was a good three to four hour job. Then, there was the washing; making curds from the goats' milk in a goatskin churn; working in the vegetable garden that yielded beans, lentils, cucumbers, leeks and onions; not to mention the endless spinning, weaving and mending!

I had smaller stitches than my mother, so my main job was the mending of clothes or sewing new ones. I was always proud of my small, neat stitches. Mother did the spinning. She would rub raw fibers of sheep's wool on her thigh, which eventually turned into a strand of yarn. We then used a heavy yarn bowl – a bowl with a small hump in the bottom that had a hole through it. I'd help her put the strand of yarn through that hole. Then she'd hold both ends of the long yarn and work it back and forth to separate the strands that I took and used for mending.

Sometimes, I switched jobs and took on the task of grinding barley into flour. It was a welcome change from my usual mending. Grinding barley took upwards of two hours. If you could ignore the ache in your wrists and ankles from squatting so much, there was an easy, almost hypnotic rhythm that was soothing. Once that job was done, add a bit of water, a fistful of fermented dough from the day previous to be used as leaven and then bake it in the oven. On festival days, mint, cumin or cinnamon was added for a yummy flavor.

I remember the first time I was asked to help with the bread.
I was six years old. Miriam gave me some barley from a storage pot.
I squatted next to her and very carefully placed my kernels between
the two basalt stones. I remember I wanted to have enough barley to
make a happy face picture. I used two for the eyes and the other five
for a nice big smile. No nose for my happy face this first time! Then
I had to work the stones together to crush the barley into a fine,
almost dusty flour. At first, I was clumsy and crushed a couple
fingers before I even dented that barley! But eventually, with
Miriam's help in gripping the sides of the stone properly, I achieved a
certain success.

I kept checking between my stones to see if I had done it
enough yet. I would show Miriam beside me, so proud of my efforts,
"Now?" I would say.
"Not yet." She'd reply…grind, grind, grind…
"Now?" I would ask again.
"Not yet," she smiled, and then playfully tipped me off balance to fall
over. Because of all my checking and pestering, I took longer than
anyone that day to grind my portion properly! When we said our
mealtime prayer that evening I had a secret smile in my heart, "Our
Father, whom art in heaven, hallowed be thy name. Thy kingdom
come, thy will be done on earth as it is in heaven, Give us this day
our daily *bread*….! A-MEN!"

Living in constant closeness, even to family you dearly love, I sometimes found myself looking for little bits of time when I could steal away to the hills. Our village was strategically positioned on a hill. We could always see any approaching visitors be they friendly or unfriendly. I would beg Miriam for a break and could she take me to the hill, please? We would walk to the outskirts of the village, and I was always extra careful and watchful. I would sit on my favorite rock while my other cousins or my brothers played nearby.

I always considered it my rock because I never saw anyone else sitting on it! It was a huge gray thing with a mostly flat top, slightly angled down. The rain had worn the edges soft and there was a tall bush that grew at one side – the perfect rest for my back. I would sit on that rock and sometimes see shepherds in the distance with their flocks of sheep. The wind would carry their whistles faintly to my ears.

I loved the wind. In the compound there was a breeze, but out on the hill there was wind! The kind of wind that you shut your eyes against and in doing so can almost see the shape of it as it blows by you. The world looked so vast and made me feel so small, and yet it was comforting, not daunting. There were many things in the world that I feared. I feared the Roman soldiers. I feared another potential miscarriage for my mother as the last one had almost killed her. But I never feared the wind. The wind was silent, but with its movements, it had character – strong and determined or soft and delicate, I loved them all.

Although we were a mid-sized village, we had a small canvasary at the outskirts of our borders. A canvasary served as an inn to house the caravan travelers during their brief stay. It was one such caravan, one very successful year for my father that things changed drastically for me at age nine. That was the year I became betrothed.

God lives in my love
God waits by my fear
Whether one or the other
God stays near

CHAPTER TWO

Caravan arrivals were always a time of excitement because they brought not just their wares for selling or trading, but also news! News from across Judea, news from Jerusalem and, of course, gossip about the latest Roman outrages.

In the blacksmith business, local iron was mined in Jordan, but the best iron came from India. If it had been a very successful year, my father would negotiate for some precious iron from India.

In trading for iron, my father ended up speaking with a group of men among the caravan. They were in the business of buying and selling camels. My brothers and I had gone with father that exciting day to see the caravan traders. We were chasing each

other when Asher shoved me into the side of one of the men. I
stumbled and fell over. I remember being so embarrassed! My
cheeks were burning hotter than the sun that day and I could not
make eye contact with the man or my father. The man picked me
up, patted me on the head and didn't seem upset with me. I
mumbled an apology and hurried back home as quickly as I could.

My reticence and heart-shaped face had intrigued the man.
He was actually a distant fourth cousin of my father's family and he
inquired about my Mohar – my bride price. It was more like a
promised guardianship of me as I was too young to truly be a wife
yet.

I had no notion of it at the time, but my young face
promised beauty. I knew many thought my mother to be a great
beauty. My mother had long curly brown hair that I often thought
looked like the wind if one could see it – waves so graceful and full
from her head to her waist. She had finely arching eyebrows and
such beautiful, kind eyes. Her eyes were brown, but close up, you
could see her eyes had tiny yellow flecks that my father teased were
gold dust.

My hair was the same color as my mother, but was mostly
straight with just some curl in the bottom of it. The still reflection

in water showed me I had the same shaped eyes as my mother. Papa told me I had green flecks in my eyes – green for my love of the hill and the great outdoors. My father's eyes were fully green with yellow specks like my mother. I always liked to think I got the green flecks in my eyes from my father. But in general, I wanted to grow up to be like my mother and have many pretty babies to keep me company. I had thought that future was far off, but life had other plans.

The caravan man's name was Jeremiah. He lived far from my home and painted a grand picture of life where his city was. His city, Capernaum, was a famous one for commerce, great markets and the camel races there were legendary. My father was sad but happy to see me go to what he considered an adventurous and prosperous way of life. Knowing how much Miriam's marriage and leaving had upset me, father told Jeremiah he must speak quietly with me before an announcement was made.

I can honestly say I had no first impression of Jeremiah from bumping into him. I hadn't even looked at him! All I knew was that he was tall and had on good quality sandals. He was just one of my father's relatives and a business friend. Beyond those minor details, he was of no particular importance in the world that existed for me at that time.

You can imagine my shock when father told me Jeremiah had asked him about arrangements for marriage! I thought instantly back to Miriam's counsel, "It is the way of every woman to marry and have children, otherwise, who would take care of her in her old age? You don't want me to grow old and be a woman on my own do you?" Miriam had settled well and when word had come of the birth of a son, I'd tried to fill my heart with only gladness. That way it could crowd out my sadness of still missing her. Now, it seemed, it was my turn.

I swallowed my fear. I swallowed my sadness. It sat like a hollow, heavy rock in my throat. I wanted to be strong like my father and obedient at all times. I wanted to make my parents proud. Stepping away from these few years of childhood was something I could do to add to their pride. *What good daughter could say no? What good daughter can stop the passing seasons of life?* It is God's will we grow and learn and stretch to our full potential as men and women. My turn was now.

Those last days at home, I tried to memorize every color, every taste and each person's face. I tucked away images like the twinkle of kindness and humor in my father's green eyes. The warm, comforting scent of my mother's soft, curly hair and how the sound of her laughter was like the tinkling bells the caravan camels wore. I even managed to steal a last visit to my father's business. I memorized the sensation of the waves of red warmth that rush out to greet you at the door - as if it had been forever since you last came and they were so happy to see you!

I was a mix of melancholy and resolve; knowing something and finding the ability within to carry through are two very different things. I took my example from my beloved Miriam and accepted this tide of change.

All my life, I've never forgotten how my mother held her tears back when she told me I would be so happy in my new home. She talked too quickly and smiled too brightly for me to really believe her so I knew her heart was crying as much, if not more than my own. How could I not mirror her courage?

It was my father who ultimately set my fears to rest. I was sitting at the table with the last of the mending I would ever do for my family when he came and crouched down at my knee. He put his hands on mine to still my stitches and told me he loved me. He told me my husband would be a good protector. My lip began trembling and the lump in my throat seemed to swell with the squeeze of my heart. I tried to hold my tears in, but by looking down to hide my face, tears plunked onto his great hands that held mine. "My little Elishva," said father and I tumbled into his warmth. I tumbled into my Papa's arms and embrace, wishing that he could always be near me.

Father held me and rocked me to soothe my tears. The deep rumble of his chest against my ear was reassuring as he continued to tell me of the good choice in a husband that had been made. Jeremiah was smart and strong and I would be living near Capernaum – imagine that! A daughter of his married and living even closer to Jerusalem, the Holy Land to our Jewish people! Papa went on to explain that the same reason Miriam had married and moved away was my own as well. Jewish families married within the same ancestor lines to keep our branch connected and strong. Miriam had to move away because there were no male relations of marrying age here from our family branch. Jeremiah's camel trading took him many places, but this would be the only time he would be passing through our area. It was a good family match and Papa didn't want me to miss this opportunity. Jeremiah's job was a prosperous one of much prestige and authority. His younger brothers took care of the family fields so their compound in Capernaum also would provide me with female companionship while Jeremiah traveled. Papa truly believed in his heart that this match was a good and happy one and I'd made him so very proud by this arrangement.

My family hosted a betrothal party two nights before I was to leave with Jeremiah and the caravan. I was very careful to wash completely clean and my mother had made a special white tunic for me to wear. My young friends in the village had painstakingly gathered whatever flowers could be found in the area for both my and Jeremiah's head wreaths.

I remember being seated beside him but did not personally enjoy feeling as though I was on parade. I was embarrassed and extremely shy. This seemed to please Jeremiah and for that I was glad. It was a relief that I didn't have to pretend to be anyone but myself with him. There was a big meal, as grand as my family could manage. Figs, olives, dates and wine flowed freely. It seemed as good an excuse as any for everyone to have a good time. Then came the moment I was most fearful of, a dance with my betrothed. His hands felt so big, big like my father's, but these were not my father's hands and I trembled. The awkwardness of the moment passed when Jeremiah tried to make me smile. He leaned down and said, "Are you not pleased with a party?" I glanced up at him and had to smile. Here was this man of dark hair and beard who looked so ridiculous with flowers in his hair! A giggle escaped me and his wide grin in return took many of the clouds from my day. His eyes sparkled and his hold on me for our dance was gentle. Right then and there I decided Jeremiah was kind. I could love this man who accepted my quiet ways.

A ketubah - marriage contract, was written and witnessed at the synagogue between my father and Jeremiah. It stated the usual marriage conditions. One agreement was that my husband always provide a home for me. Even minor details such as my yearly clothing allowance were all written down and notarized. It was typical of our custom, but I was still flabbergasted when my bride gift came from Jeremiah. I knew a gift was given to the bride from the groom as a means of sealing the contract, but when four bolts of luxurious, colorful silks were delivered to our home, I thought it was for my mother or aunt. Never could I have imagined it was for me! If it was Jeremiah's intent to impress me, he succeeded well!

Being married suddenly seemed a bright and happy life. I thought of my father's encouragement and I forced my thoughts of melancholy away. I imagined myself as Jeremiah's wife adorned in colorful silks like never before seen. I could see my future self as confident and valued as a precious gem! The silks were more luxurious than anything I'd ever seen or touched. It flowed like water through my fingers! As a budding seamstress, he certainly hit the right note with me! And like the coals of my father's business, my heart glowed in appreciation of Jeremiah's well-thought present.

I made certain to leave parcels of different colored silk for my mother and aunt to use. The rest was packed away for future use as his wife.

There was nothing left for me now but to leave and live my life in a kind of limbo until I was made a woman by God's touch and could marry and have children with Jeremiah. It all seemed so simple to me then, but life is never that uncomplicated.

Oh, Mother, can you hear my heart
It calls to you across the land
Though we may be far apart
Still, my face feels a gentle hand

CHAPTER THREE

Perhaps due to the path that life took me on, I have always remembered my last look at my family. Asher and Yakub, for once silent and still, stood at the side of my father. Mother was on Papa's other arm, holding it tight. There was much commotion and jostling as people prepared to leave and get in order for the caravan lines. Camels were voicing their protest; merchants were joking back and forth; dogs were barking underfoot, scooting here and there. I had one bundle clutched tightly in my arms. The rest of my things had been packed for travel the day before. We had all said our goodbyes at home and the walk to the canvasary had been mostly silent. I'd wanted to present myself as a young woman of maturity, but didn't resist at all when Mother took my hand shortly after leaving home and squeezed it for the rest of the walk.

Jeremiah had come to join us after ensuring his camels were in proper place and two of his employees were with them. Jeremiah spoke softly with my father. Mother put her hand on my cheek so soft and loving. Her thumb rubbed up and down and then I felt Jeremiah's heavy hand on my shoulder. "It is time," he said. Asher and Yakub hugged me. Asher made sure to pinch my arm gently, "One for the journey," he whispered and grinned. I rolled my eyes at him because I knew that's what he wanted. *Boys are awkward about goodbyes,* I thought. I dropped my bundle at my feet and gave Mother and Papa hugs. My nose pressing hard against their shoulders and I inhaled their warm scent and love. *I can breathe a part of them into my own soul. My Mother. My Father.* And I breathed them in deeply.

"Be happy, Elishva," my father said. Mother had no words for me. She just pressed her lips to my forehead firmly for a moment. Sometimes feelings are too thick for words. I wasn't sure if she heard me, but I whispered, "I love you," to her as she stepped back. Then I picked up my bundle, turned and walked away with Jeremiah.

Jeremiah felt badly for me and with our first footfall away from my family he began to point out the people he knew and stories about them to occupy my mind. I appreciated his kind attempt so gave a half smile when he told me about old Benjamin, a spice seller, who'd been tricked once into eating a small red vegetable. He'd been told it was a sweet and gnarled tomato, but was in fact a very spicy pepper that made his eyes water and he drank two entire jugs of wine to cool the fire in his throat. Jeremiah showed me how Benjamin had hopped about, crying and holding his gaping mouth…

People who have not traveled far from home have a very limited understanding of how vast the world is. When I was told it would take two months to travel to Jeremiah's home, I thought he was teasing me! *How could the world be that big?* But it was, and it did take us that long and even more.

To me, my new life was overwhelming at first. I was placed under the care of Jeremiah's cousin's wife who was traveling with the caravan. Her name was Rajeen and though she was a nervous type and always seemed to want to keep me in view, she was certainly nice enough as I recall.

Whenever I think back to that time, the colors were deceptively soft. The butter yellow of the sand was brown in its curves and shade and the enormous blue of the sky. Blue that would shimmer in its heat of the day as though an invisible sheath of silk rippled in a breeze that didn't exist and never graced our skin with its touch.

Then I remember the tastes. The taste of dust – gritty and bone dry to grind out the water in your eyes when it blew in your face. Dust and sand got everywhere. Grains of sand worked their invisible way into the folds of skin, in your ears, eyes, nose and mouth. Sand and dust found a home under fingernails and in your hair. A thing of beauty this landscape was, yet living with it exacted a harsh, daily penance.

As a watchful child with so much that was new to absorb, these discomforts just became a part of my new life, my new adventure. I quickly became friends with Rajeen's only daughter, Nazeem. She was just a year older than I and we laughed and played and walked together on the long journey. I was fascinated by Nazeem's appearance. She had vibrant red hair and eyes greener than my Papa's. I had never seen red hair before and thought it was very pretty.

We would spend our days playing and one of our favorite things was to visit the camels. We'd giggle at them behind our hands when they'd spit at us and miss. I remember we used to hold our noses and run squealing, pretending that their smell might chase us and get in our hair and clothes.

My pleasures outnumbered my discomforts and I made certain to keep busy and occupied so as not to think about my family overmuch. I missed them terribly but did my best to be and seem grateful and happy in my new life. At night I slept next to Nazeem and for me, it was a real treat. It was like having a newfound sister. She reminded me a bit of Miriam because Nazeem took me under her wing and showed me all the fun of traveling with a caravan. I'm sure for her it was a comfort to have another young girl to play with. Families often accompanied the caravans for protection in their travels, but few girls had the freedom to roam with her as I did without my parents present.

In general, it was extremely important to me to behave well. I was very conscious that I was the lone member of my family present amongst these people and how I behaved was a direct representation of my mother and father. I keenly felt this responsibility and wanted my parents to be proud of me.

I tried to take on the role of an "almost woman" with as much dignity as I could. I always made sure despite my busy playing with Nazeem to help gather water from the rivers when we camped at eventide. Rajeen was married to the merchant who sold the beautiful colors of cloth that Jeremiah had purchased as my bride gift. Nazeem showed me her exotic head cloths of intricate colors that were packed away for special stops. For traveling, we wore much sturdier linen. When I mentioned my ability to stitch neatly, I found myself helping to mend the multitude of tents in the caravan.

Besides Jeremiah's camels and his cousin's merchant business, the caravan also boasted spice sellers, oils and lamps, jewelry and fine pottery traders and makeup tradesman. It was a wonderful blend of new colors – purples, gold, silver, varying shades of greens and oranges that I had never seen before! The new smells and sounds and aromas were laid out for me, a simple girl to marvel at. I remember the first days just absorbing the myriad of everyone's accents and learning the routine of the traveling life. Nazeem would laugh at how large my eyes would get over things. For me, I was always grateful for the safe feeling she gave me in her knowledge of how to navigate our way around.

We made many stops along the way, trading for goods at various villages and towns I had heard of and never imagined I would one day see with my own eyes. Each village had its own personality, just like people. Some towns were cleaner than others, some nicer than others. Jeremiah stopped by every now and then to check on me. He was not allowed to be alone with me so Rajeen often sat in on our conversations.

During our visits, Jeremiah told me about growing up in wonderful Capernaum. His father had died in a protest against the Romans when Jeremiah was very young. His gruff manner when speaking about his father spoke volumes to my heart. Jeremiah was still hurt and felt he had been denied something everyone should have the natural right to. I knew I loved my own father so much – how could I ever imagine growing up without him? Jeremiah explained he lived with his two younger brothers in their family compound. His brothers were both farmers. They worked the family land, but Jeremiah always knew right from the start that he was destined for something different than work with his hands. He told me he started hanging around the camel races as a young boy. He chuckled, remembering the many times he'd steal away from classes at the synagogue! He'd give anything to be at the races! Jeremiah started out cleaning stables, but eventually worked his way up to become the head of camel trading. It was an enviable position. He alone made the decisions regarding the purchase and selling of the choice race camels. His dream was to one day own his own camel racing stables and I was to share in the rising of that dream.

Through our visits, I quickly came to realize how dear I was to Jeremiah's plans for the future. He said one of the first things that interested him in me was my time of birth. Being born with the rising moon of prosperity in spring was a good sign for a successful life. He had big plans and picking the right wife was important to those plans. My birth was a key factor in his choice of me as a bride. "Your birth date prophesizes your future," he believed. He himself had been born in September – the time of harvest and fresh wine for rejoicing the Passover feast. Together our birthdays equaled an unstoppable success.

It was understood that I was under the care of Rajeen and her family until we reached Capernaum. At that point, Jeremiah would place me to live with his aging mother, Rebecca and his sister, Mary, at the family compound. His brothers and their wives lived there also. For the majority of our engagement, Jeremiah would be kept busy traveling. He assured me once we wed, I would travel with him on his trading business, but until then, it was best if I were to live with and get to know his family.

Jeremiah was extremely fond of his mother and sister. Being the oldest son and in commerce, placed him in the position of responsibility for them, rather than his two younger brothers, who ran the family farms. His brothers were often in the fields and, during harvest, would set up tents at the fields and not return to the compound until harvesting was done. Jeremiah had been, "The man of the house," for as long as he could remember.

At one visit with Jeremiah, he came to me like a child; and presented in his lap, a package. I had to guess what was inside it. He told me he always made certain to buy a small gift for his mother and Mary whenever he traveled. This was Rebecca's gift and I was to try my best to guess what it was. I tried guessing cloth. No. I tried guessing spices. No. Jeremiah was pleased with my tries and his smile spread across his face with each unsuccessful guess. Finally I guessed jewelry.

Jewelry was a very fine thing for Jewish women. Only the rich had jewelry to speak of or wear. The very rich women could be seen proudly wearing a "Jerusalem of Gold" crown depicting the Holy City. My guess was correct and Jeremiah let me peek into the package to see a beautiful gold bracelet – delicate circles entwined with each other that made me gasp at its expense. I had never been so close to such wealth before! My betrothed was definitely richer than my own family if he could afford such gifts for his mother each time he traveled!

Mostly, when Jeremiah visited, he painted a golden picture of the life we were going to have together and his plans to make it all happen. I was glad he seemed to always take the direction in our conversations. My quiet nature to listen and his preference to talk made ours an easy handshake between personalities.

Jeremiah had decided once we were married, we'd travel and trade camels until our first child, (a son, we hoped) was old enough to walk. At this point, we'd be ready to purchase land and Jeremiah could start his own camel races.

Jeremiah was loyal to his employer by thinking the best possible location would be away from Capernaum, perhaps near the City of Sephoris which at that time had no camel races to boast of. Once settled there, we would live in a big house with servants and I would adorn myself in fine clothes and jewelry and decorate our house with the finest and latest furnishings.

Jeremiah saw himself in the courts of kings and with such a beautiful wife at his side and sons to come home to each night, he saw everything for us so clearly with eyes that sparkled like diamonds. He had no doubts in his mind that this was our future and he had no reason to doubt it. He had a good and stable job, was marrying a carefully chosen young girl born of the rising moon of prosperity – what was there to doubt in his well-thought out plans?

The more I listened to Jeremiah, the more I loved the life he painted for me. I could see the grand home we were to have. I could feel the joy rush through me as pictures of our sons happily running to greet their father at the end of each day decorated the corners of my mind. It was all going to be so grand and so fine a life for us.

I distinctly remember the first ripple of dissention in our picture of the future together. We had stopped at a village and I had gone with Nazeem and her family to the market for goods. That night we ate fresh food and most were content to sit and let lazy bellies lie happy. Suddenly, a man came riding towards our encampment yelling. He had come from the direction of the village and was waving a staff frantically. Before his camel had even stopped, he expertly jumped to the ground and began demanding to see Jeremiah. Waving his staff and stamping his feet, his rage was like a palpable force and I felt a curious mix of both fascination and fear. Some of the men from our camp stood and were dealing with him when Rajeen came and ushered me quickly away from the group to their tent. I looked over my shoulder and strained to hear something, anything about what had upset this man so greatly. All I heard was Jeremiah's name...a wrong done to some kind of tally...I couldn't quite hear over the scolding of Nazeem's mother; her mutters about bedtime and some other concocted excuse to get me away from "men's business." I was puzzled. Where was Jeremiah that he was not in the camp to answer to the call of his name yet? Ah, such tender innocence that the truth of the situation didn't become clear to me until years later.

I will never forget my first view of Capernaum. It was at the end of a long day of pushing for our destination. Everyone was dirty and tired, but there was a great expectation that hummed in the air. As we came over a dune of sand I saw it. Capernaum! It was getting close to the end of the day. The sun was yawning and moving out of its brightest part of the afternoon. As such, its rays hit Capernaum with the kindest light of the day, the warm beginnings of evening. When I saw the city, I caught my breath. I saw my new home bathed in dewy sparkles of pinks and soft yellows of light. It was glorious! It was huge!

This magnificent maze of modern streets and buildings was my new home? This was the place of the rich indeed! It looked as though my whole village could fit within the walls of the city a thousand times! Where my village had the meager population of two hundred, Capernaum was a bustling and busy place of near twenty thousand! I felt as small and insignificant as the overlooked leaf on a grapevine. The leaves are there, and help the life of the plant, but they are not as glorious or important as the grape itself.

Jeremiah came up behind me and put his hands on my shoulders. "Welcome to your new home Elishva," he said. "What do you think of Capernaum?"

"It is so grand!" I replied.

He chuckled and responded, "A grand city is the perfect place for our grand plans to start don't you think?" I heartily agreed. Anything was possible with such a wondrous landscape as Capernaum!

Jeremiah brought me personally to his family compound. It was different from the outset because they were city Jews, not country Jews. I met Jeremiah's two brothers and their wives, and the few small children who looked upon me with more curiosity than genuine interest. I missed Nazeem and Rajeen's presence dearly in that moment. They were stopping only briefly in Capernaum to trade and then would be moving along with the caravan to other places, as was their lifestyle.

Jeremiah's family held an overall feeling of detachment that I found discerning. But perhaps too old to be cautious of me was Jeremiah's mother, Rebecca. What an old soul she was at forty-two! She had seen much happen to our people in her lifetime. Mary,

Jeremiah's only and much beloved sister, did not like me. Her disdain for me was as immediate as our first "Shalom". Mary had Jeremiah's coloring – dark and fierce about the eyebrows. Her mouth would have been pretty could it have been allowed to soften and smile, but instead, it was disciplined and thin.

Mary gave a sour face to me when introduced, but smiled openly at her brother Jeremiah. I concluded she was just sad that I was engaged to Jeremiah. Mary was just one year younger than Jeremiah and they were very close. I think in some ways she felt her status had been hurt by my entrance into the compound and family circle. Because Rebecca's health had steadily been failing, Mary had taken on her care, and to a large degree, ruled the women of the compound - even over her brother's wives. Mary's will and determination made her seem much older than her years.

My upcoming marriage to Jeremiah would place me in a position to rival that which Mary held. Her sense of competition never made much sense to me because as soon as I married Jeremiah we would be traveling until the birth of our son, at which point, we'd settle permanently in Sephoris. I would be far from her grip of power to not interfere with it. I pondered much about Mary's instant disapproval of me and it became an endless circle from which there was no obvious answer.

The colors of my life in those years before marriage were predominantly gray. Mary used a wide brush with strong strokes to find fault in all I did or tried to do. I was quiet as a tiny, gray mouse and tried never to get in her way or earn any disapproval intentionally. My two other sisters-in-law were cautious of Mary as well and knowing how unshakable her disapproval of me was, kept their distance. They did not wish to suffer her cutting remarks or looks themselves. I could not blame their distance, but quickly felt lonely within Jeremiah's family.

Rebecca seemed to see I was an outsider and she took pity on me. With a kind look and silent manner of helping me occasionally with my tasks, in Rebecca, I gratefully found an ally in Jeremiah's family. On that massive landscape of gray where I lived, Rebecca came and stole some of it away with her kind, pink strokes.

For our evening meetings when the men went to synagogue, Rebecca would tell stories of Herod the Great. Rebecca reminded me of my father with her animated voice to tell the best stories. When she spoke of Herod, I always felt a bit sad for him. His life was the ultimate in irony - a man who tried so hard to impress both Rome and the Jews, but in his dual efforts only ended up with animosity from both. In his older years, he suffered greatly from poor physical health and a mixed mind. Just prior to his death, Herod ordered the

Jewish High Priests imprisoned and when Herod died, the priests were executed so there would be a great crying and gnashing of teeth. He wanted a show of genuine mourning from the people at his death, even if it was not truly for him!

During the time that I lived with Rebecca and Mary, I chose any opportunity to shadow Rebecca. I would lend my help with the mending when needed, but chose to spend the majority of my days grinding barley with my future mother-in-law. Young and old, we worked side by side quietly. What a pair we must have looked together. I was silent and ever watchful for Mary's approach or potential disapproval. Rebecca held an air of resignation to her aches and pains, but often with a smile on her face. She had gray hair with streaks of dark hair from her youth. Her skin was like worn leather, creases and curves that wound their way from her hairline to her pale blue eyes, down her cheeks and under her chin. Rebecca had grinded the barley all her life and was an expert at it. Sometimes she would cluck her tongue in the gaps where teeth had been, other days she would hum her favorite psalms. Even on days when her walk was more stooped and pained, she would have a smile on her face.

I asked her once if she knew a secret. "Oi? A secret? What secret is this?" she replied.

"Well," I continued, "you always have a smile no matter the day and I think it must be because you have a secret." She laughed her rusty laugh and then leaning close, she squeezed my arm saying, "A woman's source of happiness is her family, Elishva. My family might have their problems, but we are all here together! It is a constant source of joy for me to see my sons, daughters-in-law and grandchildren every day, and you too, my future daughter-in-law!" I smiled back; glad she had shared her secret with me so readily.

Sometimes, as Rebecca and I worked side by side, she would tell me stories of Jeremiah and his growing years. "It was hard for Jeremiah to lose his father so young," she began. "Jeremiah was always so different from his brothers. He played different and has always looked at life differently. Where his brothers grew strong and found connection with God's earth in farming, Jeremiah always took a different road. He never wanted the farming life. He loved the races and would come home flushed with excitement and tell us all about some race or another. To me, they all end the same – only one wins!" she laughed and clucked her tongue.

"The races are in his veins and always will be. Jeremiah lives richly, loves deeply and nothing is halfway with him. He has the heart of a winner and in you, my daughter, he sees the perfect companion to all his dreams." "Ah," she sighed, "to be young and filled with such grand plans as the two of you have. It almost makes a body wish to be young again too with the world at your feet!"

With Jeremiah's travels, he would often be gone for long absences at a time. Sometimes he would be gone for months, others just weeks separated his time from his family. Always he returned with gifts for his mother, Mary and me. Rebecca often received trinkets similar to the bracelet I'd seen, Mary received spices and sometimes a colorful head cloth, which always pleased her to wear to our evening meetings to show to the women.

For me, the gifts were most special to my heart. I'd never received gifts such as these before – jewelry similar to Rebecca that I would put away to wear once we were married. I received an orange after one trip, which was a rare, and exotic treat indeed! Mary would draw up her shoulders and proudly display whatever Jeremiah had brought for her, while I put mine away.

Always, when I heard Jeremiah return home from his trips, my heart would skip a beat. *He is here! He is home!* I sang with gladness inside. I was always happy to see him and he always had a kind word for me or praise at how I grew more beautiful since the last time he saw me.

Whenever Jeremiah returned from a trip, we would have a special meal for the whole family. The brothers would try and be home from the fields and it was a nice gathering time for everyone to hear Jeremiah tell the tales of his travels. While his little nieces and nephews kept their distance from me, they would clamor to sit in his lap for the stories he would tell.

In my eyes, my future husband was so worldly and his adventures made me long to be with him as his wife so we could see these things together. Mary would fawn over Jeremiah. She was bitter and disapproving in his absences, but with his arrival, she would radiantly smile and show her obvious love and support of him. Even Rebecca, who grew slower with age, would visibly brighten whenever Jeremiah was home. It was easy to see that Jeremiah breathed new life into this family. The excitement he brought broke through the mundane routine of everyone's existence.

For me, I would quietly stand in the shadows and watch Jeremiah bask in his family's love. Often my own heart would pang with missing my own loving family. I could not read or write; and any material to write on were purely for the synagogue's holy scrolls. The only way we could learn of each other was through the traveling caravans. Jeremiah's travels took him far, but never near my family to obtain news or provide any about me to them. So I kept faith that in time, I would be Jeremiah's wife, the apple of his eye and the partner to his happy dreams for us. And secretly I hoped we might be able to travel with a caravan back to my family at some point in our lives.

It was all coming for me soon. Jeremiah's love would fill me up. The family we were going to have would fill my days and then I would have many people around me who loved and cherished me.

I was a month away from my fourteenth birthday when my menses began. I was not surprised when they began, as my mother had discussed at length with me what to expect. When woman were experiencing their menses, we were considered "unclean". Any bodily fluid of any kind; be it blood, or fluid from the nose, open sores or wounds was considered a loss of life and immediately placed that person in an unclean state. So during our menses, we had to leave the city to convalesce at "the queen's house" outside Capernaum.

The queen's house was a gathering place for all women to wait out their time of menstruation. Being timid in nature helped because I found my menses were quite painful. It was good nobody expected conversation from me. I was able to endure my pains in silence for the most part and learned to keep my face as impassive as the other women.... I only assumed everyone felt the same pain, endured the same heaviness of flow as myself. I granted them much strength in my mind for their almost carefree manner and ability to converse in groups. I honestly thought we all felt the same physically for this time each month. It never occurred to me that we were different.

The arrival of my menses held great significance – it meant I could be married to Jeremiah, finally!

A happy bride I am today
Life smiles at us two
I'm ready to go off
On a golden journey with you

CHAPTER FOUR

Once again, my brown hair was carefully washed and parted, my eyes painted and the wreath of flowers placed in my hair. It felt so long ago that I'd had my betrothal party at my family home and now I was having my wedding day. I missed my family keenly, but without the ability to read, and the great distance between us, communication was next to impossible.

The women attending me admired the curly tips of my hair, and I was trying to explain that my mother had lovely curly, brown hair all the length of it, when Mary entered the tent. The reaction of the women was to wipe the smiles from their faces and silently finish with their fussing over my appearance. With no word to me of my bridal beauty, Mary stated, "You are late," and just as severely, she left the tent. No one dared cross what Mary said as she was Jeremiah's beloved sister.

I silently and quickly left the tent, clutching my jar of oil. I was very careful not to drop the expensive liquid as I approached the table. Many oil lamps lit the courtyard and I saw Jeremiah seated at the middle of a long feasting table. He looked so handsome and strong and my heart swelled with love. All our dreams would start this night and I approached quietly, with a smile.

Seeing Jeremiah with a wreath of flowers in his hair reminded me of my previous betrothal celebration. Jeremiah smiled back and seemed very pleased with my outfit and hair. After anointing his feet with the oil, I sat next to him at the table. "Your family was wrong you know," he whispered to me. At my questioning look he continued, "You have grown even more beautiful than your mother! You bring me much happiness this night, daughter of the rising moon of prosperity!"

Jeremiah stood and his practiced wedding line rang clear and true in his deep voice, "Behold, you are consecrated unto me." After the seven wedding messages from the Talmud were read, many stood to wish us well and give their marriage advice. It was very conspicuous as the evening continued that Mary had not offered her congratulations. I could see it bothered Jeremiah who was largely unaware of her dislike of me. His relief was easily seen when she finally stood to offer her toast. "Jeremiah," she began, "I wish you much happiness in life dear brother – now and always. You are like the sweet cinnamon in my bread at Passover. You watch out for me and I, you. You will always be my brother," at which point she looked straight at me, "whether married or not." The crowd gave the expected laugh at her comment, but I alone knew the undertone of the message. She was saying to me, "You may have married him, but I still rule the roost." If she only knew I had no desire for the power of authority in Jeremiah's household! Besides, we would be a traveling husband and wife team in the caravan. I was glad that my path would rarely cross with Mary's.

Happy was the day when I left with my new husband on the first caravan out of Capernaum! I was finally away from Mary's dominating dark moods! The only tears I shed were for Rebecca as I gently hugged her frail frame. Rebecca took my young face in her weathered hands and said softly to me, "Now, I may call you my daughter for the truth of it. Go with my heart's blessing for much adventure and prosperity, Elishva!" Her radiant smile increased her wrinkles tenfold, but the joy of her heart matched mine. I smiled into her eyes, and together we shared the secret that a growing and prosperous family was a woman's greatest happiness.

From Capernaum, we joined a caravan that was on its way to Sephoris. Jeremiah wanted to take me to see the land he had been viewing for his potential camel race location. If I thought Capernaum had been grand, Sephoris was all the sweeter in the plans we had for family and life there. The streets were clogged with the rich in their traveling carts. Servants were afoot everywhere, shouting to clear the way for their important cargo. I saw more horses than I had ever seen in my life! There seemed to be a rush for everyone needing to get here or there, sell this or that. I found it exciting, but definitely noisy!

Jeremiah delighted in showing his new bride all his favorite places and introduced me to all the right people. It was the first time I had met anyone of a higher class. Groups tended to stick with their own kind, so it was both humbling and a bit scary to meet influential and affluent people for the first time. I made certain to proudly display my fine jewelry from Jeremiah's travels and had painstakingly worked with my stitches to make fine, colorful clothes from the silks he had given me. I certainly looked the part of a young, rich bride. My vanity knew no bounds. I felt luxuriant,

radiant, loved and free from living under the pressing thumb of
Mary. My smile, those days in Sephoris, was never contrived.

I found the intensity of colors I had lived in my childhood
was now coming back to me as an adult. This golden city would
lovingly cup our growing family. I was finally married and secure in
life. I glowed with the expectation of all our happy days ahead. I
loved my husband and was beloved by him. He treated me with the
utmost concern for my comfort and I felt like the luckiest woman
alive to be so treasured! Finally, all my waiting had passed to bring
me to this joyous time of marriage! Our plans and life together lay
before us like a golden road and we skipped along it merrily; at least,
we skipped until we fell.

It was in glorious, golden Sephoris that things went sour. In
later years, I often thought of this time of my life like a soaring bird
suddenly falling out of flight - hit by a slingshot. When the bird first
begins to falter, it thinks it can just pick up speed and regain its
height. But instead, it crashes even faster to the ground. Once there,
it wobbles, hobbles, and struggles to find cover until it can fly again.
Some birds never fly again.

Word reached us that Jeremiah was to cut short his trading
journey and return with all haste to Capernaum. He was being asked

to answer to some serious financial charges. Enraged, Jeremiah packed us up and we set out that same day to return.

I encouraged Jeremiah and told him all would be well; all would straighten itself out when we returned. There must have been a terrible misunderstanding. For me, my heart sank at the thought of returning to Capernaum. Capernaum was where Mary was, but this time, I would have Jeremiah by my side. My husband would serve as a much needed buffer, and protect me from her dark moods.

Back at the family compound, Jeremiah and I were given the smallest quarters because we were supposed to be back for only a short while. It was just one room really – a rectangular shaped room that served as kitchen and bedroom in one. Other than the doorway, there was only one window to speak of and no furniture. It might have been small by some standards, but to me that was unimportant simply because this space was ours and ours alone.

Once home in the evenings, Jeremiah told me of the events unfolding at work. Someone, he said, had stolen a small portion of every trade on each camel in the last few years. It was a staggering sum in total! Due to Jeremiah's direct involvement with the trades and exchange of currencies, he was the obvious and first employee accused of the crime.

Jeremiah could not believe these accusations against him had warranted such weight. Had he not worked and toiled most of his life for the success of the races at Capernaum? Had he not abandoned his mother and sister over all these years to enable a better and more diverse herd for the races?

In my mind, I tried to calculate the cost of the jewelry he'd purchased and fine gifts for his sister and mother against the salary he received...purchasing land was expensive enough let alone the land required for racing camels...and that big home he talked of...and those servants he mentioned...it all cost a lot of money! I guess in some small corner of my mind, I, too, had some doubts about our financial situation. But as quickly as these thoughts surfaced, I shoved them back down as unacceptable! How could I not side with my husband and his offended feelings of having been falsely accused! It was a dark time for us both. Our bright dreams and hopes for the future began to fade.

In the end, the money was never recovered. There was no clear answer of who had taken it or where it had disappeared. Disgraced and dishonored, Jeremiah was demoted to caring for the daily needs of the camels as he had in his youth. I counted our blessings that at least the issue had been dealt with quietly instead of taking it to the Jewish council. Jeremiah swallowed his pride to continue working at the camel races in his demoted position. I think a part of Jeremiah hoped beyond hope that his employer would suddenly change his mind and place him back where he had once been.

Despite our circumstances, Jeremiah reassured me that our plans were only set back a little bit in time, that they could and would still happen for us. He told me he had been betting on the camel races his whole life. He promised me his luck would win out, it was only a matter of time. We would stay in Capernaum until he had won enough for us to move to Sephoris. We were confident our dreams would still happen. We just had to wait.

Sadly, this meant living in the family compound for much longer than we'd initially thought. For Mary, this situation was a mix of good and bad. She was glad to have Jeremiah home, but not under these circumstances. True to form, she managed to pin the blame of our circumstances on me. Mary maintained that after Jeremiah and I were married, I had unearthed all the jewelry and fine clothes he had previously bought me and I'd made a display of false wealth. It was this rich showing, which must have led to the rumors, and eventual accusation that it was Jeremiah who had stolen from the races to afford such luxury.

After dreaming for so long of escaping Mary's personal poison, I was stung by her accusation. The only way we were alike was in our fervent wish that Jeremiah's demotion had never occurred!

Rebecca was saddened by the events surrounding Jeremiah. I often gravitated to her in my old pattern for daily duties. She came to visit me at my quarters one day while I was preparing the evening meal. After helping her wash her hands and feet at the door, I noticed as I settled her on my seating mat that she was perspiring heavily. It worried me because it was not a hotter day than normal for that time of year. I quickly got her a cup of wine and placed it in her hands. "You are kind," she said. I gave her a moment to collect herself and waited for her to continue. "It is in my heart to defend Mary's treatment of you because I watched her grow, and in doing so, understand better the vinegar of her nature." She clucked her tongue in the old familiar way and after drinking from the cup, gave it back to me. "Why do you not participate in our evening discussions, Elishva?" she asked. "You are now married and have the right to your voice." The change of topic was so startling I had no immediate answer for her. As an unmarried young girl, my voice had not been expected at the evening meetings. Now that I was married, I knew it was my right to speak my opinions or offer my stories, but as was my way, I had not yet made any comments.

Rebecca waited for my response with the knowledge that the simple respect due an elder would bring just rewards. "I am silent because I learn more from listening," I answered honestly. Rebecca laughed her loving, rusty laugh and her eyes twinkled at mine. "You are smarter than our best donkey!" she said and I smiled back. Donkeys were for the middle-class rich and a smart donkey was worth its weight in gold. Rebecca had paid me a high compliment indeed.

"Women will find their niche in your day, just as they did in the five books of Moses," Rebecca said, "As much as the world needs men of importance, there must be mothers to give birth to them! I pray you and Jeremiah have many sons and that your sons do not forget their mother. Your father has given us a good daughter!" At this, Rebecca paused to catch her breath. I offered her the cup of wine back, but she waved my hand away. "Mary likes to think Jeremiah is hers. She is very protective of him because he has always been the only brother who ever had the patience to listen to her. Now that you are Jeremiah's wife, and hopefully soon the mother of his sons, she must grow up and learn to accept you as part of our family. Once she does, those hens my other sons married will follow in her lead. Give Mary time, she will find some new thing to be picky about and leave you in peace." I nodded my acceptance of her speech, but could not meet her eyes.

I'd blushed at her mention of children with Jeremiah. It was already five months into our marriage with no sign of children yet. I was anxious to please my husband and his family with a son. I wanted at least some small portion of our carefully constructed dreams to come true.

After traveling for most of his adulthood, Jeremiah became restless living day after day in Capernaum. He dealt with the restlessness and humiliation of his lowered status by throwing himself wholeheartedly into the politics of the day. In the evenings after the synagogue meeting was completed, Jeremiah would often come home with one or two friends to carry on discussions about the current unhappiness of our people. I would often hear Jeremiah conversing with Aaron and Canaan as they came into the compound. Knowing they were close at hand, I would quickly set out cups of wine and retreat.

Jeremiah and I still lived in the small room that served as our home and space. I would quietly sit in the corner and by the light of an oil lamp, busy myself with mending not completed while they visited. I did not want notice and did not garner any in my corner, but could not help overhearing their discussions.

Aaron, I personally thought, resembled the bellows my father used to blow air into the coals to make them burn more brightly. Aaron was a lot of wind with little backbone to actually fulfill his big talk. He even looked a bit like the bellow too, I thought. His hair was cropped short and he wore his beard trimmed neat and fine. With such short hair, it only emphasized his wide girth and made my comparison to the bellows an easy one.

If Aaron was the bellows, Canaan was like the coals themselves. He had a strong upper body from his work in the fields. His hair was dark, but his beard was mostly red. Canaan was filled with fire and easily voiced his outrage at the injustices against our people. I believed Canaan would have made a good Macabee. The Macabee family was greatly revered by the Jewish people. Known for their bravery and passion of faith, gladly would Canaan have joined those rebels of historical times who charged lands and made men into Jews by forced circumcision. Canaan revered our gory past and was by far, the scarier of the two friends.

"The signs are making themselves known," Aaron said. "The signs foretold that show the coming of the Messiah!" he continued, "These insolent Greeks infest our land like the locusts Moses set on Egypt."

Canaan not to be outdone, eagerly added, "I tell you, God is punishing us for our tainted ways! God's punishment calls every male Jew to overthrow this heathen Roman Empire!"

"But do you truly believe John the Baptist could be our Messiah?" asked Jeremiah.

"He is of King David's line, he appeals to the masses, and he baptizes us in the name of the Lord – what other sign do you need?" asked Canaan. "The time is ripe for our glory – two generations have we been underfoot, I tell you, the time is now with John the Baptist!"

Everyone knew of the royal David line. I say "royal" because to Jews, they truly were our royalty. King David's line was always watched closely for any chance of a coming Messiah and a return to power. Many Jews counted on David's line for deliverance from the Roman Empire.

Royalty had its privileges, too. Being of a higher class in society, they received a higher level of education than most, and some of that education came from special Essene villages. Qumran was the main Essene compound by the shores of the Dead Sea. There were other compounds of lesser importance scattered about, but Essene villages could be found in various places throughout greater Judea. They were filled with the families related to David's royal line.

Essene priests had ruled alongside King David while he was on the throne. Once David's reign was overturned, the high priests retreated to the countryside at Qumran where they lived in isolation. These priests kept themselves separated by distance and by choice from the goings on of the Roman Empire. They remained untainted by the Hellenistic ways that quickly sprouted like weeds over the fertile land of Jerusalem. John the Baptist was of David's line and his family lived in an Essene village.

I feared my husband's fervor would eventually get him into trouble, and I was most sadly right.

A wolf in sheep's clothing is still a wolf
No matter what it wears
But a wolf cannot credit itself with a soul
That already has its tares

CHAPTER FIVE

For my husband, the offended passion of his standpoint only
increased after an event at the market. There was a protest. Aaron,
Canaan and Jeremiah participated. Pontius Pilate ordered his
soldiers to dress in Jewish clothing and mix randomly among the
crowd. In their clothing, the soldiers hid swords and when they
were all in place within the people, the soldiers began to viciously
cut the Jews down. The soldiers did as they had been commanded,
striking protestor and bystander alike. It was a huge, bloody rabble
and my husband was one of the protestors injured.

I will never forget the terror of my heart the day it
happened. I was gathering our drying clothes from the rooftop of

our home when there was a great shouting and I saw a small crowd of people rushing along. "The Romans!" they wailed, "The Romans have cut us down!" My heart beat faster at the thought that Jeremiah had gone that morning to protest in the market area.

Frozen stiff with fear, I watched the first of the crowd rush by our compound entrance and breathed a sigh of relief. But then, I saw Aaron stumble in and he called, "Elishva! Elishva!" I snapped out of my trance of terror and never in my life did I descend so quickly down the ladder from the roof! I ran trembling up to Aaron as close as I dared, "Where is Jeremiah!" I cried. Mary and other family members joined me at the entrance to the compound and murmured their questions and concerns at Aaron. Above their commotion he cried, "It is Jeremiah! He has been injured by the Roman soldiers! We were protesting....soldiers were hidden among us...they brandished their swords and swung left and right at us – women and children too – it mattered not to them!" Tears ran down the cheeks of Aaron and shock had given his eyes a glazed look. I gave him a quick, cursory glance and saw he was mostly unscathed. I saw just one cut on his right shoulder that bled.
"Where is Jeremiah!" cried Mary.
Aaron caught his breath and said, "They are bringing him as fast as they can." What color might have been in my face, drained into God's earth at my feet. Was Jeremiah so wounded he could not walk

on his own? Or like his father before him, was it his dead body they
were carting back for burial?

Mary screamed her frustration, "Aaron...!" but was cut off by the
shouts of others at the open doorway. "Ho! It is Jeremiah! Bring
help! Where is Elishva? Where is Mary!" I instantly called back,
"We are here!" at the same time Mary called,

"I am here!"

We both rushed forward and I saw two men carrying a limp
Jeremiah between them. He was bleeding heavily from a cut on his
head and there were numerous cuts on his legs. Bruises were already
beginning to show on his face and arms. I noticed one of his sandals
was missing. "He's lost a sandal," was my mundane thought amidst
the chaos. "Bring him to my quarters!" demanded Mary. I felt my
mouth drop open in shock. "Hurry!" she commanded, "This way!"
They had only gone two, shuffling steps when Rebecca was suddenly
standing in their path. "Take Jeremiah to his own living quarters,"
she stated quietly. Mary immediately made motion to protest, but
Rebecca struck her walking staff impatiently on the ground and
Mary had no choice but to bow her head.

"Follow me!" I said, and hurried without looking back at
Mary for her reaction. Who cared about her power issues when
Jeremiah needed immediate care! They laid him on our seating mats

and Jeremiah let out a low groan of protest. "Praise be the God of the Jews! My husband is alive!" I sang under my breath.

The men left as quickly as they'd come and I immediately lugged one of our water jugs closer to Jeremiah. I took my full basket of mending pieces, dumped it quickly and one by one wet the strips and laid them over the wound on his head. Then I tenderly covered all his cuts with wet strips and gently removed the one remaining sandal from his foot. I retrieved one of the winter blankets and laid that over him as well. Then there was no more that could be done.

I sat beside him and held his hand, feeling helpless. I knew Rebecca would see to calling the priest, as to when he might be able to come was unknown. There would be many calling for the healing priests now.

A shadow darkened the door, but I did not look up from my gaze at Jeremiah's face. Mary knelt on the other side of Jeremiah and viewed my handiwork. "He is breathing," she stated. Her voice spoke the softest I'd ever heard.
"Yes." I replied.
"Will he make it?" she whispered.
I looked up then and saw my own fear mirrored in her eyes.
Without Jeremiah we were defenseless women. Certainly, she had

her other brothers and cousins, but none concerned themselves with her well being, none were as close to her heart as Jeremiah.

For me, I would be completely destitute. As a widow I would remain for the burial, but then would be returned to my family in disgrace, a widow, no children to recommend me. I had failed to bear a son or daughter to raise. No son to care for me in my old age and no daughter to keep me company. As a childless widow, I would become a burden to my own family. Because I had not successfully had a child in my first marriage, very few men would consider my looks important enough to overlook this major flaw of female infertility.

I honestly don't know how long Mary and I sat staring at each other, fear pushing our thoughts through the wall of animosity between us. Our ears listened keenly for the sound of Jeremiah's labored breathing, in and out, in and out. If a heart can will a body to breathe, I believe Mary and I helped sustain Jeremiah in those moments.

Rebecca came to the door to see how I was doing and broke my gaze with Mary. Jeremiah's mother knelt slowly next to her son. She smoothed the bloody hair from his forehead and began to croon an old lullaby she had sung to him as a babe. Tears coursed down her weathered cheeks and my heart broke for each of the women in that room.

All of us loved Jeremiah in our own way. What would become of us if he died? Poor Rebecca must have been reliving the day they brought her husband's broken body home. And so, we three sat and waited and prayed...

Two weeks later found me filling two water jugs in the middle of the day. Normally, water would have been collected much earlier – and I had done that, but our need for water had increased. Jeremiah had healed and was sitting now, but his ankle had been damaged. It pained him still and he was able to hobble only short distances. The cut on his head continued to give him headaches, but he was alive and mending and we were all so grateful for that.

Many had died that day in the riot...so very tragic, especially the children. There had been so many burials the professional mourners were double booked to lead the wailing processions to the burial grounds! Everywhere one looked there was the evidence of ash rubbed on cheeks for someone who had died.

For us, it had taken only nine days, which seemed like months, for a Jewish healing priest and his assistant to arrive for

Jeremiah. I had to leave our home while they tended to him. Tired of the silence of his convalescence day in and day out, Jeremiah was eager to tell me all about the priest's visit after they had gone. He said they brought their long case and after saying a prayer at the door, and the ritual washing of their hands and feet, entered our home.

They had the usual few things to help Jeremiah with his pain. I listened, fascinated, as Jeremiah described the long case they had brought and pulled forth a long stick of some kind. Using some special water they had brought themselves, they mixed a bit of the stick with the water. Working both together, the priest made a paste that was applied to the scab on Jeremiah's head. Then with a nod from the priest, the assistant brought out a vial of oil and handed it to the priest. After reading the inscription on the bottle, he smiled and nodded his acceptance of the choice. The assistant then recited a healing prayer under his breath as he anointed Jeremiah's head and ankle with the special oil. Last but not least, before they made their exit to the next one who needed help, they offered Jeremiah a scroll.

Scrolls were given only to those who could afford them. They contained specific passages from the five books of Moses. The scrolls were special talismans of healing. Because papyrus for writing was a rich thing to have, these scrolls were indeed special to us. I was proud and so pleased that we could afford one such scroll for Jeremiah. Surely with the words of our Lord residing in our own home, Jeremiah's successful healing would take place.

Jeremiah was very proud of his scroll and always kept it on his lap or in his hands. None were to read the inscribed words but him and despite his immense pride in them, he was not allowed to tell anyone what the inscription said. They were for him and him alone.

I was happy that the visit and the healing had gone so well. Jeremiah's face shone with genuine appreciation of their talents and life was sweet again.

So there I was, gathering a second round of water for our daily needs, despite the midday heat of the sun. As I approached our quarters, I could hear voices and was glad of the company. It had been five days since the uplifting visit from the priest and again, Jeremiah quickly grew bored with his convalescence. Visitors were always welcome as a distraction from the headaches and pained ankle.

I stepped inside silently and set the large jar next to the door. "Elishva!" called Jeremiah, "Aaron has come to visit!" I immediately stifled my impulse to frown. I disliked Aaron and did not want him in our home. True, he had brought word to us first of Jeremiah's condition, but I could not help feeling he was partly to blame for encouraging my husband's presence at the riot that day. Canaan had been in the fields that day and had missed the entire protest and its violent conclusion. He had visited Jeremiah and lamented his absence that day and Jeremiah had proudly displayed his wounds for his friend. Now at Aaron's visit, I merely nodded and poured a glass of wine, diluting it with fresh water for him.

Fear struck like a bone needle in my heart as I heard the direction of their conversation. This time, they were debating the recent issue of Jesus. Jesus, like his cousin John, was born of David's line. John had been beheaded the month previous and the country had waited three days expecting him to rise from the dead and bring about the new age of the Jewish people. When that didn't happen, the frustrations of the people incited the riot where Jeremiah was hurt. We all knew a Messiah was prophesized for our people from David's line, we just weren't entirely sure who that Messiah would be.

Jesus was the latest relative being heralded as the possible Messiah. But the Jewish people placed Jesus in direct conflict with his own brother James for the lofty position of Messiah. Depending on your point of view, it was easy to discredit one for the other as Messiah and vice versa.

     My husband easily chose James. Jesus offended Jeremiah for many reasons – his birthright being the main one. Royal families had different marriage rites than the rest of the classes of society. Their marriages had a three-step process. First there was a betrothal period. This lasted at least a year to publicly "claim" each other as potential partners. After the betrothal year was done, a trial marriage took place in September. This was a strategic choice because September was the time of our Passover feast and was the holiest time of the year. Then, in December, two months later, the newlyweds could begin trying to conceive. During this first trial marriage, if the woman became pregnant, the couple waited until her third successful month of pregnancy, when a second, life-bonding marriage took place. The timing of this was crucial because a baby conceived in December would be born the following September. A royal baby born in September could be the prophetic Messiah.

     If however, the woman was unsuccessful in carrying her baby and miscarried, the second marriage wouldn't take place. The couple had three years to try and birth a child. If a child never came, the first marriage was dissolved. For David's royal line, the betrothal and trial marriage meant nothing; it was only the second marriage that was considered fully legal and life bonding.

Jesus was conceived while Joseph and Mary were betrothed – that is, Mary was a virgin and became pregnant before her trial marriage had taken place. Simon Boethus was in position as Jewish high priest at the time of Jesus' birth nine months later. Simon did not believe in the prophecy that a Messiah would be born of David's line, so he punished Mary for her intimacy with Joseph prior to their trial marriage by deciding she had to give birth to her child in the unclean Queen's House. She retreated to the Qumran Queen's House, also known as their "manger" which was located an hour's walk from the compound and served as their housing area for animals.

Of course, Joseph and Mary did continue with the steps – they had a trial marriage and then also a second marriage celebration to fully bond them for life. It was after this second marriage that another son James was born. So who was the official first son with the heavier mantle of David's line on his shoulders? Was it Jesus, born in a manger? Or was it James, born within the full legal acceptance of their marriage?

Currently, Jonathan Annas was the high priest and he fully accepted and put forth Jesus as the Messiah. But my husband was not so easily swayed. Jesus had been gone traveling for some time and had come home with very odd ideas. He didn't seem to hold any fire, any animosity towards the Hellenistic Greeks or the Roman Empire. He had even been quoted as insulting the Pharisees about the length of the fringes on their clothing! My husband couldn't believe Jesus would openly mock that which demonstrated the Pharisee's level of holiness! How God did not smite him for this blasphemy must only be because of David's blood in him – or so my husband believed.

Jesus' brother, James was more my husband's kind of leader. James was of the common, favored idea to take Rome by force - to fight our way through and vanquish our enemies as had generations upon generations of Jews before us.

I felt my heart stutter in my chest at the direction of Jeremiah and Aaron's conversation. I doubled resolved myself that I must bear Jeremiah a child. A child would give my husband something besides politics to think of. A child would fill his life with laughter and more love. More love in his heart would leave less room for this growing discontentment I saw in him. My mind was made up; my body had other plans.

Can a flower hold hope?
We can only guess
Every petal is a promise
But God knows best

CHAPTER SIX

It was a joyous day for me indeed when Mary finally married. She was considered very old by our standards for marriage, but had found an amiable match in an older cousin whose wife had died, leaving him with a young daughter to raise. Like Mary, her husband was bitter about life in general and oddly their combined bitterness brought them each a certain happiness. *Another irony of life!* I thought.

Jeremiah was not pleased with Mary's marriage. He wanted his sister close as she had always been. Life was changing too much from the picture he had always envisioned for himself.

Jeremiah had lost his job and now was losing his only beloved sister. And, she was moving to Sephoris!

Prior to the riot, the gambling had been going badly and we were worse off than we had ever been financially. Jeremiah's heart broke, as did his voice, when he gave a toast at Mary's wedding feast. It was hard for me to watch Jeremiah struggle with his heartache. We were both watching the color of our dreams fade further.

After Mary's marriage, Jeremiah healed completely and went back to work and back to trying his luck at the races. Life after Mary left was definitely more peaceful for me, but I merely shifted my worries to another area. Without having to constantly think about avoiding Mary in the compound, I spent my time worrying that I had not gotten pregnant.

All my prayers for a child had been fruitless and Jeremiah grew daily more bitter about his life. He sorely missed his previous authority at work. Where he had once been a trusted buyer, he was now more an observer, no longer delegated to even voice his approval or rebuke the caravan's choice camels. He sensed that others were often laughing behind his back and it enraged him.

As the days went on, his gambling losses mounted higher. Mary was gone to her new, prosperous life in Sephoris. She would have children like he should have had. As much as you can be happy for someone you love, watching them live the life *you* want is hard.

Jeremiah felt he was drowning in life's disappointments – like a covered pot that comes to a boil over a fire, his spouts of steam were beginning to bounce the top and make it dance darkly. I always knew when he'd had a bad day. He said little, ate his food as though he was angry at it, and I learned that silence is always best when faced with moods such as these.

With Mary's absence, I took on the care of Rebecca – her mending and washing, preparing her meals and each night I helped tuck her in with blankets. Rebecca's condition worsened after Mary left despite my best efforts. The healing priests were brought in to see her, but nothing seemed to help her. Rebecca watched her family with a sad heart. One did not need eyes to see the changes taking place.

One night, Rebecca seemed to gain back some of her lost strength and as I was about to get her blanket laid out for her she asked me to sit for a moment. "Child," she began, "I remember the day Jeremiah brought you here to our home. You were so young, so quiet! I knew from my first look at you that you had a good heart inside." She took my hands in hers and I made certain to rest my hands gently. Rebecca's skin had grown painfully thin and I didn't want to bruise her. "I can see the pain it causes you that you have not had any children yet. Take heart, dear daughter! Think of the great women from our books of Moses! Hannah prayed for seven years to give birth to Samuel! It will happen for you! God answers the prayers of a faithful heart, Elishva, but His time is not the same as ours. Think of Hannah and keep your heart pure in prayer." She raised my hands in hers; and after placing a kiss on the palm of my right hand, she placed some purple flowers on it. My eyes widened in surprise when I saw them.

In Rebecca's endless kindness, she had purchased some purple mandrake flowers from the healing priests that could be boiled as a tea to drink. Mandrake tea aided a woman's ability to conceive a baby. She smiled at my surprised expression and gave a low chuckle as she pointed to a fist-sized bundle in the corner of her room. It was a bag full of mandrake flowers for me!

I have never forgotten her words or the hope she gave so selflessly to me that night. I remember leaving her quarters with a smile on my face and in my heart. God had answered my prayers through Rebecca and her kind offer of the flowers. *Surely now, I will become pregnant and my long wait will be over. A baby! These flowers will help me have a baby! Praise God for Rebecca, Praise God for the healing priests and Praise God for answering my prayers!* I thought. My night was filled with sweet dreams of children's messy faces and scraped knees to tend to and I loved these pictures that painted their vibrant, happy way through my mind.

The next day was to bring me even more joy. While setting the unleavened bread to bake in the oven, I heard a woman's voice at the entrance of the compound. "Elishva?" asked the woman. I turned, confused, no one ever visited me, who could this be? But as soon as I saw her, my heart leapt for joy. "Nazeem?" I cried and ran laughing in my shock towards her. She too came rushing and we embraced with tears soaking each other's shoulder. "How do you come here? How have you been? Is Rajeen with you? Are you still with the caravans?" Nazeem laughed at my questions and we took a step back from each other, just holding hands for a moment to reevaluate each other and the years added to our appearance.

Nazeem's red hair was just as red as ever, and her eyes danced in the same way. The lines that ran from the corners of her eyes only enhanced the impression that she had sparkling eyes like stars. And her clothes were so beautiful! The colors of her head cloth were like a sunset bursting with warm oranges and yellows.

Her tunic was made of soft silk, orange to match the head cloth, but the neckline held fine, fine stitches that played in intricate patterns around the entire tunic. Gold jewelry adorned her neck, wrists and ankle. She was a vision of beauty and my heart sang its happiness for her well being.

"Elishva you look wonderful!" said Nazeem and I blushed and looked down at our feet. I knew she was lying for the benefit of saying kind words to me. Wanting to change the direction of our greeting, I immediately invited her to my quarters for tea. Setting the water to boil we went inside.

I was proud that my home was neat and tidy, but it certainly lacked the grandness she must be accustomed to and I was embarrassed I could not offer her even a chair to sit on. "These mats are so beautiful Elishva, did you make them yourself?" asked Nazeem. I nodded proudly and we sat together on the blue/green woven seating mats Jeremiah and I used. "You always were so good with your needle," said Nazeem and I smiled at the memory of my time with her.

"How is it you are here today Nazeem?" I asked.
"This is the first time I have traveled close to Capernaum since my mother and I left you here with Jeremiah. Ah Elishva, isn't it

amazing how life can thread its way down such unexpected paths?" she asked. I nodded and she continued, "After we left you here, my father's silk trading business took us through Jerusalem. I met a young man named Reuben there from my mother's side of the family. I kept traveling with my father and the caravans but always Rueben stayed in my mind. When we went by Jerusalem two years ago, we met again and I ended up marrying him! Settled life is so different from traveling with the caravans. I missed it so much, we decided to help father out this past year as he is aging and having some difficulty." I sat and watched the sun radiate out from my childhood friend. Her skin was glowing, her eyes were shining and with all her gold, she shimmered. I felt my own heart lift with her happy tale and my own smile at her was radiant.

"Elishva," she leaned close to me like in the old days when she had some mischief on her mind, "I visited your family six months ago with the caravan," she said. Her laughter at my shocked expression was full of her happy mischief. "Nazeem! How are my parents? How are my brothers, Asher and Yakub? Did you learn anything of Miriam?" I urged her on to tell me everything. She gladly related all that she could remember.

Mother was well and kept busy leading the women's group for the village in the evenings. Father's business had been going well and Asher was continuing on at the synagogue to learn more. Yakub was father's assistant and would learn the family blacksmithing trade. Of Miriam, she had four children. Her fifth child, a little girl, had tragically died of fever at just a few months old.

I felt my eyes swell up with tears at the images of my family and their progress in my absence. I wondered if father's beard had begun to gray or what mother looked like now. I raised my hand to feel my cheek in remembrance of her last, motherly touch.

Yakub going into the blacksmith trade did not surprise me. Asher continuing on in the synagogue did though! I wondered if he pinched any of the priests there and the thought made me smile.

I took Nazeem's hands and thanked her for the news, such sweet, sweet news after years of wondering about my family. It was beyond wonderful to now have some updates on their whereabouts and lives.

"And what of you Elishva?" asked Nazeem. "You married Jeremiah and then what? I thought to find you in Sephoris, but instead you are here." I looked down at our hands and pulled away, thinking of what I was going to say. "Yes," I answered carefully, "I married Jeremiah when I was fourteen. We did go to Sephoris after we married, but came back when there were problems at the races here. Jeremiah is still sorting things out. His mother has grown quite frail and his sister has married and moved away so I have been taking care of Rebecca," I paused to gather a breath and some inner strength before I said, "We have not had any children yet, but I have some tea now that I have been drinking and we are quite hopeful." I looked at Nazeem with my last comment. My eyes shone with my earnestness and my hopes. "Ah Elishva," said Nazeem softly, "I am sorry you are having trouble. Is it mandrake tea you are drinking?" she asked. I nodded. "Then let us have some!" she proclaimed, "That water will have boiled itself out of the pot by now Elishva! Let us get our hot drinks!"

Nazeem stayed for two hours. Two very precious hours where we laughed over memories of spitting camels and l listened to her stories of adventure from her caravan years. I lived a lifetime of happiness in those hours with her; but at the same time it felt like only seconds since her arrival when she stated she had to be going.

The caravan she had been traveling with hadn't even stopped at Capernaum. She had broken from the route to come and visit with me and now her two escorts would accompany her safely back to join the caravan before the afternoon was done.

She promised to take news of me back to my family at the first opportunity she had. We hugged and squeezed each other goodbye and the tears began again for us both. "Elishva, take good care of yourself," she said. "You too Nazeem. Be happy with Reuben and good luck getting back safely to the caravan. Thank you again so much for bringing me news of my family! It means the world to me!" I told her.

"Ah Elishva! Look at us! We are crying out all the tea we just shared! Go now and make yourself another cup!" she laughed. I watched her ride away with her two escorts and thanked God for a friend like Nazeem, then, I turned and went back to the necessities of my day with a lighter step than normal.

I first went to check on Rebecca and tell her all about my visit with Nazeem. I had introduced my friend to all of Jeremiah's family in the compound when we got our tea. Rebecca was happy that I had news of my family and had seen an old friend. The rest of the day passed uneventful. It was two nights later that Rebecca died peacefully in her sleep.

Bruises are purple
Welts are red
Thoughts are reaching
For dreams in my head

CHAPTER SEVEN

As Rebecca's main caretaker, I took on the task of preparing Rebecca's body for burial. Tenderly, I washed her frail body with both water from the jugs and my own tears. Rebecca had always been so gracious to everyone, especially to an outsider like me.

After washing her body, I anointed it with sweet smelling spices and dressed her carefully in white burial wrappings before she was placed in her wooden coffin. We sent word with the next caravan to Mary, but there was no possible way she could travel fast enough from Sephoris to be present for the burial march. The professional mourners led the way with their wails; but since Rebecca was the main residing elder in our women's evening group, the tears were certainly genuine for those of us following the procession.

We took Rebecca's coffin to the small family cave. She was placed inside the cave and would remain there for a year; at which time, her bones would be collected and put in a special ornate box. There were many boxes of ancestors kept in the family cave.

As much as my heart broke for myself, it broke, too, for Jeremiah. With his mother's death, he became more withdrawn from me and where I had always enjoyed his endless conversation, I now found a sullen man as quiet as myself.

Two months later when Mary was able to come and visit, Jeremiah brightened considerably. But Mary, true to form, used the visit as an opportunity to throw dirt my way. "It is interesting that all the while I cared for mother she was fine, but under Elishva's ministrations she died." I was shocked by her bold accusation. Jeremiah quickly jumped to my defense, "Now Mary," he said, "mother had been sick for a long time and we all knew it...your leaving caused her much sorrow of the heart as it did for us all..." His voice trailed off at the end and I bowed my head with tears of anger and humiliation. Jeremiah might have spoken the correct words, but his conviction could not be heard in them.

Mary was like a dog that had finally found its buried bone and couldn't be more pleased with herself. All along she had thought I was an intruder of the worst kind and here was her proof. Jeremiah was finally coming around to seeing me the way she did and when opportunity knocked, her door was wide open.

It seemed then that sadness was destined to always live with us and in the midst of it all was me, his wife – his childless, tea-drinking wife. Mary's doubts and criticisms replayed themselves in Jeremiah's mind like a mantra of the soul, "It all began with her...when you got married you lost your job because she wore that jewelry." Then his own doubts would tag along after, "Because of her, Mary moved away...when Elishva cared for mother she died...." Round and round the thoughts turned and somehow their repeating pattern made them easier to believe.

On a seemingly normal day, Jeremiah came home from work and I set the dish of warm food between us. After giving thanks to our Lord and taking his first mouthful, Jeremiah slammed his bowl down in frustration and some of the food splattered on his tunic and beard.

Even in it's retelling, my heart beats like the wings of a fleeing bird... wings flapping on each rung in a cage that offers no escape. With a roar he picked up the entire dish of food and flung it against the wall. "THIS WILL STAIN MY BEST TUNIC!!" he raged and picked me up in fistfuls of cloth. In some part of my mind, I knew the hand he'd pulled back was going to swing into me, but I refused to believe it.

There was a moment of disorientation for me as I fell from the blow. I remember the jolt from landing on the mud packed floor so hard. These physical things register in your mind, but there is adrenaline and shock running a thick race in your veins and the wild sensation of self-preservation kicks in. I stayed on the floor in a helpless bundle and covered my head with my arms.

My husband channeled his anger, frustration and raging strength on me. The bitterness, the jealousy and the injustice of his life flowed like a churning black river through him. I was the obvious and only safe harbor for all the reasons why life was not as he deserved it.

This first outburst was brief. After a few kicks he seemed to truly see me crumpled on the floor, he gave a strangled cry of anguish and ran out the door. In his absence and with the immediate danger gone, I began crying. *My kind and loving husband, this is not in your heart! This is all an accident! A terrible accident!* I thought.

Trembling, I was crying in earnest at my husband's sadness and frustration, crying for my arms empty of a baby. After all this time, I was crying also for my own gentle, kind father and crying for the comforting arms of my mother.

As I sobbed, I automatically began cleaning up the mess. How I desperately missed my beloved Miriam, family and homeland. I wondered if Nazeem had been able to take my news to them yet. Despite the years, I liked to imagine them looking the same as the day I last saw them, healthy, young and strong.

Despite the pain, I managed to salvage some of our supper. Life is relentless like that sometimes. No matter how the soul craves a break in time, the wheel grinds along in those moments of despair and we have no choice but to follow its call.

I washed my own face, hands and feet to cleanse myself again. I did a thorough job of it too as if I could wash away the evening and its events…and then I waited, sitting quietly and patiently at my spot on the mat in case he returned. I did not attend the woman's meeting that evening. I waited for the return of Jeremiah. Night came, the stars bloomed full in their garden of richest night, and I fell asleep waiting.

In the morning, I woke stiff with a tender eye, sore shoulder and a headache intense enough to match my fear. I snapped up in my spot and saw my husband at the door. He had returned, changed his clothes, placed a blanket over me at some point and was looking over his shoulder as he left for work.

We, each of us, blinked at the other. The room was silent, heavy with tension. My heart swelled in fear and love and it called to him – *Oh my Jeremiah! I'm so sorry for your pain! I want to make your life better so you would never be so sad and angry again! I would give you the son of my heart if only the body could hear my prayers! I would give you back your old job and all the respect of the world! I would give you your life in Sephoris and your mother alive and well! I would give you it all if I could!* I waited. I trembled. He seemed to want to say something, but turned and walked away.

In my land, in my time in history, it was the law that a husband could discipline his wife as he saw fit, but my father never beat my mother. He had always raised laughter in her rather than bruises.

I remember going through the daily chores that day with a constantly stuttering heart. I was restless, and an uneasy anticipation of my husband's return walked with my every step. I kept thinking about the evening to come when talk would be taking place between us again.

His shadow darkened the bowl I placed on our supper mat and I quickly looked up to see him. The fast movement made me wince and I was glad I'd worn my full head cloth to hide the worst of the bruise and swelling at the side of my face.

Jeremiah cleared his throat and sat down. After prayers we began eating quietly. The meal, for the most part, was silent except for a few nondescript comments about the races. He never mentioned whether he won or lost that day with his bets and I did not ask. At the end of our meal, he said he was going out to the synagogue and that was it. The day after was done and I breathed a sigh of relief. Yet, despite my fear of him, I felt lonely without him.

Life took on this pattern of repetition for me. I would watch Jeremiah gather in anger. He was like a farmer collecting grain from a plentiful harvest and I never knew when he would have enough bushels gathered to burst forth and spill his fists on me. All the while I kept praying for a baby. All the while, I kept drinking my tea and thinking of Rebecca and Nazeem and my family. Thoughts of them helped keep my mind from what was happening to me.

The beatings themselves were like living someone else's life. It felt unreal to me. At my worst, I think he saw much of himself in me in those moments. I was helpless as he was helpless in his life. I could do nothing about the pain being inflicted upon me; I was like a tiny boat caught unawares in a quickly rising storm on the Sea of Galilee.

And the yelling. I remember him yelling. Words that hurt my ears and shook my body. I was lowly, unworthy of him! How laughable I was to think I could ever truly be a wife to him! Where were his sons! Where was the prestige I was to have brought him? Where was my rising moon now? Where was his prosperity! I had done nothing but ruin his life! Ruined his chances! It was my entire fault! All his troubles came down to this useless, lazy, thing he called his wife! How could I have done this to him? How could I have crushed his dreams with my vanity! How could I have taken his sister and mother away! Didn't I love him? Wasn't he worthy of the best in life? Why was I not giving him what he deserved! I was the vessel of his dark days and rarely the recipient of any lighter moments.

As the years passed, my bones began to slow in their response to my instructions. I noticed I was growing weaker. My nails now were brittle and would often break in my daily mending. I lost my appetite and began eating less and less. Even my hair, once young and heavy, thinned out and became as brittle as my nails. How could a bruised and broken body house a baby? My heart split so at this thought; still, I kept a constant vigilance of prayers and thoughts of Hannah's success.

As we approached our sixth year of marriage, my beatings ceased completely. The time of my menses had always been a painful, heavy experience for me. My heart would plummet at the arrival of my menses. Again, I had been unsuccessful at conception. I felt a mother's calling inside that echoed in a chamber hollow of a baby's cries or a child's laughter.

In spite of my failing health, I tried to keep my face to the hope that God would answer my daily prayers for a child. But suddenly, in the middle of my normal days between menses I began to bleed unexpectedly. It was as though a sleeping demon had awoken within my body. The demon clenched at my stomach with its claws and blood flowed like a river. I tried to stop bleeding. I clenched my legs together. I leaned heavily on the wall of our home as I felt my knees weaken, but any effort I made was useless, still the blood came. My last bit of strength took wing on the echo of my cry as I fell to the floor of our home.

Later that day, Jeremiah found me on the floor. I lay sprawled in a pool of blood and his first thought was that I had been murdered.

Could I have seen this coming?
Prevented my demise?
God uses every evil
As a good thing in disguise

CHAPTER EIGHT

Jeremiah's anguished cry as he rushed to me brought forth others who gasped in shock and then horror as they realized I had not bled from the hand of another. They quickly retreated – they could not afford to be tainted from an unclean room. Word was sent on flying feet for a healing priest.

Five days later, before the beginning of the Sabbath, none of their healing oils, pastes, or blue kohl on my eyelids had helped. I continued to bleed sporadically. As an aid, we had purchased a sacred scroll of written words.

I could not read my scroll, so the priest kindly spoke the sacred passages to me to remember them. They became a constant litany in my mind to shut out the aching pain. "Whoever goes to the Lord for safety can say to Him, 'You are my defender and protector. You are my God, in You I trust.' He will keep you safe from all hidden dangers and from all deadly diseases. He will cover you with His wings; you will be safe in His care; His faithfulness will protect and defend you."

I could not stay in the housing quarters on the Sabbath in my bleeding state. By mid-day, I was moved to a small room in the compound, next to the animals. An unclean woman, placed in quarters next to the unclean animals. It was in this room I was to live out the next four years.

Of my time in history, there was a clear distinction of classes that was strictly observed. As a woman, I was born on the lower rungs of society. At the time of my menses, I was lowered another level. But by becoming sick, I would be thrown out of even my current class of married women. For someone who is sick and unclean, the penalty is complete isolation from your people.

An unclean person cannot and must not touch anyone or anything of any kind of value or they would taint it. For instance, if

I was to touch or carry a jar while sick or in an "unclean" state, the laws decreed that the jar would have to be destroyed. Any substance in the jar – be it wine or water would be thrown away. If anyone was to have drunk from an unclean jar, they would require purification rites – a seven-day sequestered time of repentance, cleansing by running clean water and a dove sacrifice offered at the temple.

If an unclean person was from a poor family, they were cast out from the village boundaries to live in the wilderness by the pagan Hellenistic healing ponds. It was a cursed class. Any person with a major illness was viewed as housing an evil spirit for some sin or some rule disregarded... this was God's way of striking at those who did wrong.

We were not poor enough for me to be outcast from the family compound. It would not look good on the family name to "throw me away" as it were. So, as was often, in middleclass families of some financial means, I was kept segregated within the compound.

I was now one of the unclean class. The blood came, and I was segregated from my people. There were times of mad hunger that came. It was like crawling worms, crying in protest, as they seeked the corners of my stomach for sustenance. I fought this mad hunger because it held the strange urge to eat the dirt I lay on. Eating dirt?

When one is displaced, such change is harder for the mind to accommodate than the body. The body reacts almost immediately to any new environment – if you go from a hot to a cold place, you shiver. If you go from a dry to a wet place, you seek shelter. The needs of the body in search for well being shift immediately. But the mind is not so easily moved.

Those first days, I denied pain its space in my mind by thinking of all the tasks of life's routine. The unleavened bread that was sitting in the corner would go bad if not worked with in the next two days. The mending on my husband's tunic - specifically the hem at the back that was starting to look worn needed some stitches. The water in the morning – who was going to provide the fresh water each day at our quarters for those to enter?

Now that I was officially unclean, what would happen to my house? Would the priest deem it and anything in it unsalvageable and, therefore, tear it down?

I had no idea of what was going to happen to my home or the things in it – they were essential to our daily life. If destroyed, we would have to purchase them again upon my return. I would need my mending basket and needles, our jars for water, cloth to cover the leaven bread for baking each day. How long would I need to stay under the running water for this seemingly endless occurrence of sickness? It might take more than a dove for sacrifice to fully cleanse me when this was over.

Worries spun in my mind like cloth, enough to clothe an entire Roman army. But worry helped pass the time and at first it shut out the pain as nothing else.

I scoured my mind for the ritual or rule I had overlooked that had brought this misfortune upon me. I desperately turned a blind eye to the obvious – I had not given Jeremiah a son. Jeremiah's words would haunt my ears without the effort of his own breath. *I was lazy, I was unworthy, my own dear, sweet father had lied to Jeremiah by telling him I had been born with the prophetic rising of the moon, I had brought only disgrace to his life, I was unworthy of him and this was my own punishment, my own yoke to bear with none to blame for it but myself…*there were so many hours in a day to spin my own personal haircloth.

Jeremiah and various family members came to look upon me in my small area. I could sometimes hear their muted tones talking about me and preferred not to listen if I could help it. I was like some new oddity in their home and they came to see the "tainted one". If I chanced a look at them, they'd scurry away or pretend to have been looking in on the animals. As much as they were curious, they were fearful of eye contact. If eye contact was made, they themselves might be afflicted with my sickness.

Nights were the worst. Without the bleating of the animals or the sounds of life in the courtyard, there was only silence. In this silence, I would lay drenched in sweat and sleep eluded me though I was more tired than I can ever recall. I would feel lightheaded and want to vomit at the same time. Chills would come and go at their own will.

I learned much in that time of my life. I learned there are waves of pain that you cannot crawl away from. Pain deeper than sound or color, pain that cages you and drives you mad. I embraced agony as though it was the only friend I had. Like a shawl placed around a huddled form to provide warmth, pain was all encompassing and shawl after shawl was placed over my quaking body. And I fully accepted each shawl. I grew accustomed to feeling their weight in such contrast to the emptiness I felt inside.

These days of endurance
Must surely soon be done
I crawl round in my darkness
Searching
Where can be the sun?

CHAPTER NINE

Jeremiah's younger niece, Dinah, was given charge of caring for me. Everyday she would shove shreds of material to me with a stick. I would leave my bloody, soiled bits in a bowl just inside the entrance. She would come to collect the bowl and then it would be burned everyday. Every morning, a new stick was found to push a bowl of food towards me and so forth. But it was rare that I would eat anything at all. The pain stole my appetite and wore at me like a grinding stone.

Dinah was a kind girl with a streak of the rebel in her. The unenviable task of caring for me was her punishment for sneaking into the synagogue – she could have been stoned for such an affront! Caring for my needs was seen as fit punishment.

Because Dinah was bitter about this decision, she would sometimes come and sit in the animals' quarters and as she milked the goats, would talk about what was the newest, juiciest gossip around. I lived for Dinah's daily milking time and her words gave me something, anything to pour all my energy into focusing on. My ears perked up especially when she mentioned Jesus.

Jesus, it seemed, was causing quite a stir. This man was speaking to the multitudes about finding the Kingdom of God within and not needing to buy one's way into salvation with sacrifices and rules! I was especially interested in the healings that Jesus had performed. He was working his way across the countryside healing lepers and sick women!

I thought back to Jeremiah's conversations with Aaron and Canaan. I knew Jeremiah was against Jesus and all for James, but Dinah never told me stories about James healing people. Thought had taken root in the fertile ground of my despair. A thought the size of a mustard seed planted itself in my soul – so impossibly tiny that mustard seed, destined for incredible growth.

I began to fill the hours of every day with thoughts of Jesus and the stories of his miracles. *The Messiah is among us and his name is Jesus! This man Jesus is like the wings of God that will cover me and protect me from disease like the scroll says!*

I wanted to leave my rotting isolation to seek out Jesus, but I could be stoned to death should I even try to take one step beyond my room. Despite the obstacles of my situation, the mustard seed of my faith grew strong and I knew without a doubt that Jesus could save me! *I must get to Jesus!* It became my obsession – the balancing counterpart to my pain.

Then one day, Mary visited. Dinah shocked me with the news that Mary had come to visit with her two daughters. *Her two daughters?* I thought. *I remember her husband only had one daughter to raise…when did Mary have a baby? How long have I been living in here? How old is this daughter?*

Dinah mentioned Mary was pregnant again and she was gloating. That certainly sounded like the Mary I knew. It surprised me when she came to visit. She made sure to stand a good space away from the entrance of my room. "Look at you now," she sneered, "You have finally revealed your true self! Did you know? They say the End of Days is upon us, Elishva." I was sitting, leaning against the wall, and looking down at my hands as she continued, "You know as well as I what that means for you. Hell will be your home for falsely misleading Jeremiah into marriage! They say Jesus is the Messiah. Did you hear me? The Messiah is among us! When God raises the dead and separates the good from the evil, you will be the one that burns in hell because the demons in your body make you bleed. I hate you, Elishva for taking my brother's future from him and killing my mother! Do you hear me, Elishva?" Without thinking, I instinctively looked up at her to indicate I'd heard her and she gasped just as we were about to make eye contact. *Am I that gruesome to look upon?* I thought to myself at her look of horror. But then she puzzled me further by clutching her stomach protectively and rushing away.

I knew in my heart Mary was right. Jewish people were very much hopeful of the coming apocalypse. After generations of persecutions, occupation of our holy land by the Hellenists and living under the oppressive Roman Empire, the time was ripe for God to bring the Day of Judgment. Many thought that our time was near when God's angels would descend from heaven. They would raise the dead from their graves and every man would be judged and go to heaven or be banished to the fiery pit of hell for eternity. The Messiah's coming meant he would bring the End of Days. For any who were not pure, they would be cast down to hell.

I was still contemplating all this when I heard crying in the courtyard. A scurry of feet and then one of my sisters-in-law yelled, "Elishva! Look up, Elishva!" I slowly did as I was told, curious through my pained haze as to what the new disturbance was. My sister-in-law shrieked at my countenance and cried as she ran away, "It's true! There are sores by her mouth! Oh Mary! Poor Mary was right!" My heart dropped like a stone and I heaved as I realized what had happened.

Open sores that appear on or about the mouth of one woman, was believed to cause miscarriage among other women. The crying continued in the courtyard and I knew Mary must be experiencing problems with her baby; problems with her baby that everyone would now believe were caused by me.

I put my hand over my mouth and felt the small wounds at the corners. I tried to think in my mind, *When did these happen? Was it today or some other day and I just didn't know?* I honestly couldn't answer my own question. I had no idea when these had appeared. But the date of their appearance mattered little. The fact they were noticed on the day Mary miscarried was another damning mark against me.

Jewish marriages lasted at the very least, ten years. By law, a Jewish man could divorce his wife, if after ten years she had not borne any children. My segregation and onset of my bleeding illness began during my sixth year of marriage. The days plodded along. One after another. Pain today. Pain tomorrow. Blood today. Blood tomorrow. Mary's miscarriage occurred in my ninth year of marriage. She encouraged Jeremiah heavily, with the aid of her husband, to petition the Jewish High Priest for a divorce before I killed them all.

Given my status, Mary was certain Jeremiah could convince the priest for the divorce and thereby return me to my family – as was outlined in my marriage contract. Jeremiah was agreeable to this but some small corner of his heart felt guilty that perhaps his treatment of me had weakened my body enough for the demon to enter it.

I felt the presence of someone before they spoke. "Elishva?" he said. I looked up only slightly, in hope that Jeremiah had come to visit and offer words of comfort or encouragement. In my vanity, not wanting him to see me in such a dirty state, I only turned my head to look out the doorway, but would not dare look at him directly. Jeremiah's breath caught in his throat. I was grotesque in my pain. The sickness had left me as an old woman. The only part of me with any fire of life was the mantra that played itself over and over in my heart. *Jesus saves. Jesus saves. Jesus saves. Jesus saves.*

Jeremiah cleared his throat and pushed on with what he had come to tell me. "Elishva, I have decided to try one last time to heal you. I have sent for the temple healers to come with their oils and scrolls...I want to help...I...I want to try one last time...if this doesn't work, Elishva, I am going to draw up the papers to break our marriage contract. It's been almost ten years, Elishva, and I've no sons...You...you are too sick to do this...to be...They will begin coming tomorrow to administer whatever help God grants them."

I feel my fire pushing through the muck of me! This is urgent! "Jesus saves!" scratches my voice. "What is that you said, Elishva?" asked Jeremiah. My voice croaking like an old toad I force it to work again for me, "Jesus saves! Jesus saves! Jesus saves! JESUS SAVES!" I finished with an almost yell. Jeremiah took a step back as if struck. His eyebrows drew together like storm clouds feeding off one another. "Jesus?" he says, "Jesus saves the poor and weak of mind! Jesus is no Messiah, Elishva – he cannot help you! If you want a Messiah, it is James I tell you! Jesus plays with his parables to confuse our holy priests. What kind of Jew is that? I will not have this upstart Jesus in my home do you hear!" Jeremiah's voice carries loud and it strikes my ear but I do not hear him. "Jesus saves! Jesus saves!" I moan.

"No, Elishva," says Jeremiah, "Jesus does NOT save and will not save you! I will not send for him. He will not come into my home! The healing priests will come. They will do their best for you."

So Jeremiah made his last effort to try and heal me. He sent money and contacted all the healing priests available to come and try their ministrations again. They all accepted his money. They all came. And they all failed. With each fresh failure to help me, I fell further into my fervor. Jesus saves. Jesus saves. Jesus saves...

Bearing the brunt of life's burdens
My shoulders stoop so low
My bones cry out for eternal rest
And echo my heartfelt woe

CHAPTER TEN

When I became engaged to Jeremiah, my mother told me to think of our lives as if each of us was a feather. There are times when we lie still and silent on the ground and there is little change in our routines. Then, by the breath of God, we are carried up and away – change occurs and takes us somewhere new. Sometimes that change is chaotic, it scares us, and we frantically twist as though helpless, but God's plan for us is perfect. We may not understand the why or where we will end up to rest again, but it is God's breath that moves us to our destination.

Mother taught me there is never a destination without its purpose for us. In those dark years, I often thought of myself as a twisting, frantic feather and longed for the peace and silence – to be a feather on the ground. But in my pain, I reminded myself that God was merely breathing me to a new destination, helping me reach a greater height of self that would not have been possible without that feather's flight.

Day after day in my room I became convinced in my mind, in my heart, with *all* that was in me, I knew Jesus could save me. If I could not get to Jesus, I would die. I knew these thoughts were blasphemy to my husband. But I thought them anyway. I already felt like I was dying. But I continued to live. *Why don't I die? Why am I still here? Perhaps I am already condemned and this life is my hell. I have failed everyone I loved so much. I have failed you all. My life in this stinking room is my punishment and I am damned. I am damned. I am damned….. but Jesus saves. Jesus saves. Jesus saves!*

I would spend hours thinking of my rock that Miriam used to take me to. I thought of Hannah and of children. I thought mostly of the wind. I thought of the wind in my hair and closing my eyes against its movements. I remembered its gentleness touching my skin. I remembered my skin so healthy and worthy of the wind.

But the pain invaded such happy memories. Pain was the demon eating my happy thoughts and laughing with its full belly of my lost hopes. My lost life. My lost everything....

Then...I barely noticed a voice speaking. It had been a long night and I was too tired to think straight. But yes, someone spoke to me. It was a male voice. I was instantly afraid it was Jeremiah coming to tell me we were divorced. *I do not want to hear him!* But no, this voice was not Jeremiah's.

I slowly opened my eyes. I saw an angel in the doorway! Robes of purest white! *I was not worthy! I didn't want to go to hell!* I buried my face in the dirt, so ashamed! I was burning with shame! *My face that once promised beauty was shrunken and pale. My eyes that fully sparkled at my father's stories were now bluish and empty. My hair and nails were brittle and dirty. I was soiled. I was damned!*

In desperation, I began stuttering the scroll passages in the hopes my faith might save me, "Who-whoever goes to the Lord for safety - You are my defender and protector - He will keep me safe from all dangers. He will cover me with his wings; I will be safe in his care. Jesus saves. Jesus saves. Jesus saves!" Then the angel leaned down and spoke to me slowly and clearly,

"I am not Jesus. My name is Daniel. I am an Essene priest from
Qumran, Elishva. I was sent to help you with your sickness. I might
not be Jesus, but I know him." At this, he caught my full attention
and I opened my eyes to see him and listen.

This man knows Jesus? I thought. He was crouched beside
me so closely that I tried to curl myself away more so as not to touch
him and taint his holiness. He might be an Essene priest, but to me
he was as pure as an angel and I didn't want to touch him to make
him dirty. Everyone knew the highest-ranking priests were the
closest people to God.

"Elishva, I cannot help you at this stage," Daniel smiled a kind smile,
"but you mentioned Jesus." My eyes widened! Daniel continued,
"Yes, Jesus. He is a gifted healer from God. He has healed the blind
and the lame. He can heal you where I cannot." At this point,
Daniel looked to the door to see if anyone was standing, listening.
Then he said very quietly to me, "Jesus will be on the road to
Capernaum this afternoon. Go, Elishva, and be healed. God has
heard your prayers. Jesus heals."

The dirt of my hand meets
The dirt of your robe
With you, each of us
Can unburden our load

CHAPTER ELEVEN

I was kneeling along the well-traveled dirt path to Capernaum. I silently sat in a position which pressed my body against my knees, bowed in reverence with my nose and forehead touching the dirt. There must have been over a hundred of us there. Some kneeling on their knees along the path, others like me are full on the ground in a show of humbleness and reverence. We all waited for one man. Jesus.

I think briefly of my painful journey here. I had struggled to sit when Daniel told me to seek out Jesus. I was determined to do his bidding, though leaving was going to be tricky. I had not used my legs in so long I was not sure they could be relied upon to take me where I needed to go. Daniel ordered the compound to empty of all inhabitants for his healing and cleansing time with me. No one would think to question a priest and they all left as told.

Daniel placed his hands over and above my body. Then without touching me, ran his hands in the air along the length of me. I felt a slight easing of my discomforts. He then procured a head cloth for me and gently tucked my matted hair into it. He swung a long and wide shawl over me to hide the state of my tunic and gave me a strong walking stick to help me. "Keep your head low and walk like an old woman," he instructed. I almost had the energy to smile, looking old would be no effort on my part. This wasted body would have no problems giving the impression of age.

My heart pounded in my chest as he helped me leave the compound. *His faithfulness will protect and defend you.* My heart rammed itself against my ribs. Daniel helped me travel out of the city while I looked only at the ground and thanked God for this stranger's help. It was not far from the outer walls that others had begun to mill about to find their position on the path. Daniel helped me kneel and then quickly left so as not to attract too much attention my way. When he first helped me kneel there was no one else about me. Time passed and now there were many others just like me. We lined the path like so many paving stones – a mosaic of needs in each of us wanting to see Jesus.

I worked in my mind how best to go about this. I had decided the only part of Jesus I would touch would be his sandal. I reasoned it would be the dirtiest part of him. From walking, his sandal would be covered in the dust of the road so it would not be like touching Jesus, I would be touching only the dirt that was of Jesus. I didn't want to taint him with my own uncleanliness. If I could just touch his sandal I will be healed! I knew with every breath, every blink of my eyes, every part of my being sang with this truth. Such was the power of Jesus our Messiah. My knees and legs had long since gone numb. It will not be long now I heard others murmur along the line. Anticipation was on the rise.

My heart leapt to my throat the instant we heard the distant commotion of someone coming along the path. My heart clamored so loudly I feared the person crouched next to me would tell me to be quiet! Or maybe my guilty thoughts of what I was about to do were screaming so loud in my own head, they could be heard by Jesus himself and he would accuse me before even reaching me! But no - I held my breath - Jesus was approaching. *Jesus! Oh Jesus! My only hope! Jesus saves! Jesus heals!*

I concentrated on my hearing to make sure my timing was just right. I listened with keen eagerness as they walked closer and closer. I could hear the disciples talking amongst themselves and a kind voice was saying, "Thank you, my child," and, "God bless". Footsteps came closer and closer and as best I could time it, I snuck a peek up just barely and saw his feet! It was Jesus' feet! His sandals were brown leather – expensive and sturdy. Sure enough, there was a thin coat of dust from his footfalls on the pathway – that dust was all-important; the only remotely permissible part of Jesus I would dare touch! My heart was pounding, "Jesus saves. Jesus saves." But at the last second I hesitated! *This audacious woman is not me! How DARE I, a woman so beneath him even THINK of doing such a thing?* My hesitation cost me dearly. The opportunity to touch his sandal was gone! A footstep – Jesus' footstep was gone while I hesitated! *All is lost!*

My soul cried, "NOOOOO!" In despair and panic I quickly decided my last chance was to touch the dusty hem of his robes! Jesus wore a robe of white – good quality material with a burgundy colored braid sewn along the edge. Even a small thread colored like gold, so pure yellow, ran alongside it. I despised touching any part of his fine clothes. *I am so dirty! He is so clean!* But my desperation to NOT touch Jesus is stronger! *If I don't touch him, all is lost!* My hand shot out! With his steps forward, the burgundy braid and a bit of the white material flutters over my hand like an angel's wing. In the instant I touched Jesus, I felt a ribbon sizzle quickly down my arm and into my belly! At the startling sizzle, I quickly dash my hand back tight to me.

I feel different already! I have done it! I have touched Jesus! The pain is gone! The demon is out of me! The bleeding has stopped! I am healed! I can have a baby now! I will not be in pain anymore! Oh glorious God! I am saved! Oh Jesus! Thank you Jesus! Wonderful Jesus! Jesus has saved me! My heart is pounding wildly with elation! But then Jesus stops a mere step past me, and asks, "Who touched me?" Just like that, my elation dropped to terror! Scared for my life, hugging the offending hand deep in my chest to hide it, protect it, I tried to melt into the person to my right. Some others to my left called out, "It was that woman there!" I broke out in a cold sweat. *They will stone me for sure!* I despaired!

Immediately, Jesus' disciples rained their criticisms upon me like thunderbolts, "How dare you! Don't you know this is Jesus?" In shame and terror, I kept my nose firmly to the ground, my eyes squeezed tight and my offending hand buried deep and protected. And despite the immediacy of this awful situation and potential death, I remember I had a smile so deep – a secret smile all my own – my salvation – my healing moment with the true Messiah! I had reached across our different classes and claimed my salvation in Jesus! Even if they were to kill me now, no one could stone away my healing or kick it out of me. It was mine forever!

I felt a hand on my shoulder and I shuddered. If it was possible, I tensed even more, thinking this hand would be the one to pull me up and present me to the crowd for punishment. Or perhaps such was his heavenliness that Jesus would immediately cast me into the burning fury of hell itself! But to the contrary, Jesus' voice came from above me, "Leave her alone," he said, "this woman believes. None of you can boast such faith." Then he said softly, just to me, "You are healed." I began sobbing in shocked gratitude and disbelief! His kindness in the face of my boldness somehow made me feel more ashamed than ever! I never dared look up; I could not look up even if I wanted to! I was still terrified of the disciples and of the crowd that was accusatory.

Jesus and his disciples walked on. I heard the crowd about me disperse in wonder at his mercy on me. I heard someone spit and a stone was kicked towards me that bumped against my hip, but I just waited in my humble position, eyes squeezed tight, hand buried deep and began to explore within myself this feeling of newness, a feeling almost of being lighter than air with the burden of pain banished by Jesus.

I waited a long time until I heard no more mutterings or footfalls around me. I listened as the crowd followed Jesus and all about me gradually gave way to silence. Only then did I slowly get up. I kept my head bowed low, eyes only on the ground at my feet and tried to hide my offending hand in my robes. I walked slowly away, leaving my earlier old woman's walking stick abandoned on the path, but I wanted to run! I tried to seem humble but my spirit was flying! I felt alive as I had never felt before! Every bit of my body hummed and sang praises to Jesus! *Jesus! Praise Jesus!* I felt like laughing and hugging every bush and tree I crossed.

I chanced a look at the sky – how blue and beautiful it was! The blue was bluer than any blue I'd ever seen! The ground seemed to pulse with its own heartbeat - *Praise be to God*! The flowers that sing and the grasses that smile when we are born were shouting, "Jesus is here among us!"

I had lived in black darkness and pain for what seemed an eternity to me – what fresh air was mine to breath now! What happy thoughts coursed through my mind like never before! What a joyful, bright light I felt inside me where there had only been emptiness and pain! *Jeremiah! Oh! He will be so pleased! I can have a baby now! I can feel my body is healthy as never before! We don't have to get a divorce now! We have a second chance at all those lost dreams we once planned! Anything is possible in Jesus!*

I laughed at the shocked look on everyone's faces when I ran through the entrance to our family compound! I laughed at the women's gasps and laughed even harder at their shrieks when I stepped closer to try and hug them. I grabbed the stunned hands of Dinah and danced in a circle with her and kissed her cheek yelling, "Thank you, Dinah!" for her years of selfless service to me. "What has happened? The Essene priest healed you!" cried Dinah. "No," I sang, "Jesus! It was Jesus! The rumors are true! Jesus saves! I touched his cloak on the road to Capernaum and now I am healed! I am healed! " I laughed with tears of joy in my eyes.

Then I raced to my quarters to find Jeremiah. I saw a table and chairs there – *what new furniture is this? We must be gaining in finances for these luxuries! Oh, glorious day! I can see us at our table eating and Jeremiah bouncing a baby on his knee!*

I twirled around the new table and sang my heart's praises to God. I raised my shining face to the heavens, unwrapped my head cloth, and palms up I twirled and twirled and praised God! I stumbled to my knees and laughed like a child at my clumsiness. I rocked and laughed with newfound life. Tears of joy could not be contained! Everything could be had in this life now!

When I opened my eyes, I saw Jeremiah's feet in the door and my heart skipped a beat. I lifted my face to tell him the good news but before I'd even gathered a breath to tell him, he gripped my chin and thrust his face in mine. "So!" he roared, "it is true! Just look at you! They told me you went and saw Jesus!" Carefree in my joy, I could not possibly bottle it up. "Yes!" I sang and smiled. I prayed for the newfound love and joy in my heart to reach out and fill my husband's heart too – *if only he could feel Jesus' love like I have, it would not matter what position he held in the classes of life. God's love is all we need! Only faith! How I want to share this with him! If Jesus can touch lowly me, surely he can bring Jeremiah up as well!*

My innocence and hopes were misplaced. My husband had just come from the temple, the divorce papers in hand. In fact, Jeremiah had already arranged for marriage to another woman, a widow who carried with her a sizeable amount of money. His "new life" without me had taken much time, consideration and heavily borrowed funds to convince the woman to marry him. He wanted her wealth. It would bring him back to the life of prestige and respect he'd had before me. His new life did not include me! Yet again, I proved opposite to his plans. I had gone against his command and went to Jesus.

Jeremiah might have called in the healing priests, but he had fully expected to divorce me or that I would die. He had played the part of the grieving husband well. He was furious at my interference against what he wanted in life yet again!

The slaps of old, rained down on me. For the first time, I did nothing to protect my head or my belly. Somewhere, in a remote corner of my mind, I knew he was yelling the same tirade of insults at me, but I did not hear him. I was truly lost to him. Where there had been a demon with all-encompassing pain, was now an angel of light. Because I had touched Jesus, it made me pain-proof to Jeremiah's cruelty. I felt nothing. Nothing but the pure joy and love of God! I was so filled with that precious miracle fresh from Jesus that there was no room for pain. Even as my husband wrapped his thick fingers about my neck, I was smiling because I could see heaven behind him.

If I thought the colors of the world were beautiful, heaven's brilliance was tenfold. There was a white light that held all kinds of beautiful colors in it – shimmering, glimmering, welcoming, loving – it called to my soul and I joyfully ran to it. I could hear angels singing and I knew I was going home to heaven. This feather had found its final resting ground.

Epilogue

When I think now of how I was born on a rising moon of prosperity, I am humbled that my moment with Jesus became one of his many miracles in the Bible. I was just an ordinary woman, an outcast who suffered from too little meat in my diet resulting in severe iron deficiency. But from great pain, can come great miracles. It took many dark hours for me to fight for my own worth.

Jeremiah, I am sad to say, never remarried. News of my death reached the ears of his intended bride who shunned him. I always saw Jeremiah with kind eyes and felt sorry that his well-laid plans never happened for him.

Without a sense of accountability, Jeremiah was a frantic feather in flight. He fought life's circumstances with all his strength. Jeremiah didn't understand that life is about flowing with grace, especially amidst the twists of the wind!

I myself may not be able to boast much grace in my hours of turmoil, but if forgiveness is divine, I hope we all have some small spark of that in us.

Author's notes

This book was written based upon two dreams I had in 2005 of this woman's life. I researched what I could of Jewish traditions in the time of Jesus to write as accurately as I could; please forgive me for any inaccuracies described and for those details or rules I just plain don't know! That's the beauty of fiction – it gives allowances to the author where necessary!

The character of Elishva is widely thought to have suffered from hemorrhaging or "bleeding problems" for up to 12 years prior to her encounter with Jesus. I have written her as having iron deficiency (which includes bleeding problems) and base this theory on a skeletal sample taken at Herculaneum. It was destroyed after Mount Vesuvius erupted in 79 CE. Testing showed that 41% of the women suffered from abnormal bone-marrow space and porosity, indicating high levels of iron deficiency. At the time of Jesus, many

Jewish families only ate meat once a year at Passover. Very little meat meant very little iron supporting their systems.

To any historian reading this book, I must note one main change I purposefully made. Capernaum, at the time of Jesus, was mainly a garrison town for the Roman Empire. Soldiers used this place as a rest stop on their way to outer Judea postings. It was an administrative center and not the bustling city of civilians I have written it for.

The viewpoint regarding the three-step marriage process for David's royal line was inspired by Dr. Barbara Thiering, a theologian and scholar based in Sydney, Australia and her book, *Jesus and the Dead Sea Scrolls*.

Although Elishva endured much abuse at the hands of her husband, her final courage enabled her to take action. She bravely struck out to do something for herself – even though it held the very real punishment of stoning. I hope any woman who has suffered (or is suffering in) an abusive relationship finds that inner courage to seek help for herself. Every person and their body are worthy of respect – be they woman or man.

To contact women's shelters in Canada, or the US, please visit my website www.gingertsang.com for links, suggested reading group questions, previews of upcoming novels or just to drop by and say hi!

Selected Bibliography and Source Material

The author wishes to thank all those whose invaluable work is listed below.

Browne, S. The Mystical Life of Jesus. New York: Dutton, 2006.

Browne, S. The Two Marys. New York: Dutton, 2007.

Lamsa, G.M. The Modern New Testament from the Aramaic. Tennesse: Lightning Source Inc., 2001.

Reader's Digest Association Inc. The Story of Jesus. New York: Reader's Digest Association, 1993.

Reader's Digest Association Inc. Great People of the Bible and How they Lived. New York: Reader's Digest Association Inc., 1974.

Thiering, B. Jesus and the Riddle of the Dead Sea Scrolls. Toronto: Doubleday Canada Ltd., 1992.

Vamosh, M.F. Daily Life at the time of Jesus. Israel: Abingdon Press, 2001.

Vamosh, M.F. Women at the time of the Bible. Israel: Abingdon Press, 2008.

If you enjoyed *The Woman Who Dared Touch Jesus*, turn the page for a synopsis of Ginger Tsang's next two novels, *Essene Story*, based upon Daniel, the healing priest who helped Elishva find her way to Jesus and *The Languages of God: Pella's Ponderings*.

Coming 2009

Essene Story

From Ginger Tsang's first novel, *The Woman who Dared Touch Jesus, Essene Story* is the life journey of Daniel, the Essene healing priest who encouraged Elishva to seek out Jesus.

From his abandonment outside Qumran as a newborn, to his life within the compound, we follow Daniel's escalation in their strict hierarchy and levels of secret knowledge. Because of the circumstances of his birth, Daniel is hungry for the respect and adoration of the position of high priest. His one rival to power in Qumran is a fellow student named Gershom.

After Gershom suffers a freak accident, Daniel is catapulted into power and finds his success not as fulfilling as he'd always dreamed. When Jesus comes to learn at Qumran, it is Daniel who learns the true meaning of life and takes Jesus' counsel to heart. Not able to reconcile himself to the philosophy and rules at Qumran any longer, Daniel abandons his post and the only home he's ever known to go forth in the wilderness to serve the people.

This is the story of internal struggle, intellect versus listening to one's heart and finding that all the knowledge in the world can't fill a hungry soul.

Coming 2010

The Languages of God: Pella's Ponderings

After translating the hidden scrolls of Daniel's life in, *Essene Story*, Pella, a modern-day, top paleographologist, takes some time off work to research the languages of God. Her search for what seems elusive, leads her down some very surprising paths she could never have foreseen.

www.ingramcontent.com/pod-product-compliance
Lightning Source LLC
Chambersburg PA
CBHW051922240626
47153CB00004B/1326